HE FUMBLED

HER HEART

A Novel by

Brittany Nicole

To submit a manuscript for our review,

email us at

<u>submissions@majorkeypublishing.com</u>

Acknowledgements

First and foremost, I have to thank my Lord and Savior for bringing me this far. Man, the last few years have been a rollercoaster for me, but God got me through it. A few years ago, when I started my writing career, I thought I was going to take off, and it was going to be a breeze. Well, life said otherwise. God allowed me to start when I did, but it wasn't the time for me to shine. Now, He's giving me another opportunity, and I'm praying it's my time to shine. I'm ready to put in the work that I didn't know I had to put in the last time around. I'm so thankful for a second chance, and as long as God is on my side, I can't fail.

This is book number five for me. I'm not up there with the people in the double digits but just give me time. I'm going to get there. I have stories that play in my head like movies, and my pen stay ready to apply pressure. I'm not like most writers that research things to write about. I write about what I know. Things I have encountered most of my life. That hood niggas, the hood rats, the good girls and the good guys. I appreciate those that enjoy what I write about. Ya'll the truth!

Along with the fact that this is my dream, I do this for my babies, CJ and Christian. My amazing five-year-old and my happy eleven-month-old. Both my babies came at a time in my life when I needed them most. God literally placed them in my lap when I needed more love. They depend on me for a better and loving life, and I got them no matter what. Mommy loves you two more than anything in this world, and every single thing I do, I do it for you. I am forever determined to do what I need to do to make you proud and have the understanding that mommy will break her neck for you two.

Shout out to my brothers and sister. It's been established that WE ALL WE GOT!! What's understood don't need to be explained. Being the FIVE children of Laverne Green, is everything to be proud of. I love you!

Shout out to my sister, Nicole… The reason I was named Brittany Nicole. I love you, sister. For everything I could mention and everything I could possibly forget to mention, so I won't even try. You were second in command, after Mama, now it's just you. My kids and I can't thank you enough, and we can't love you enough, but we can try!

I have to say thank you to my publisher, Jahquel J. For being understanding and guiding me on my story line. Giving me the advice to make me better is how I always envisioned a publisher helping me. I appreciate you, sis. I hope you know how proud we are of every accomplish you make. When you're winning, we're winning. Your hustle makes us want to hustle. We grinding right there with you.

I am dedicating every single book I write to my guardian angels in heaven, my parents. It's been eleven years since I lost my daddy and six years since I lost my mama. Being without them has been the hardest thing ever, but I swear I know they're looking out for me in heaven. Every struggle I endure and every highlight I experience, they were right by my side every step of the way. I love them so much, and I miss them just as much. I know they would be so proud of the woman and mother that I have become. I intend to continue and make them even more proud.

I also have to thank my kids' father, my best friend, and my other half. Thank you for being a big part of my support system the last thirteen years. When I told you I was writing again, you encouraged me. You never let me feel like I couldn't, and for that, I'm very thankful, and this is my way of letting the world know you the shit. LOL!

This will be my first book on Major Key Publishing, and I am so excited to really apply pressure in this literary world with this great company. Special thank you to my publisher Quiana Nicole. In such a short time, you've shown just how hard you go behind your authors and it was really needed. I can't wait to learn so much from you and make proud moments.

Man, let me tell ya'll. 2019 had some man ups and downs. The biggest blessing I experienced was the birth of my second born. When I found out I was pregnant with him, I didn't think I was ready for another one. It's real when they say God giveth and he taketh away. I had lost my job, I developed terrible anxiety, but I was abundantly blessed with everlasting love from my baby boys. In 2019, I was hurt, I was betrayed, I was talked about, I was lied to. Many days, I cried myself to sleep. I swear, I didn't know which way was up. I couldn't tell anyone, because the words wouldn't come out. I was so lost for the longest. Writing bought me back. Being given this opportunity gave me a light I thought was forever lost. I say all this to say, embrace the hardships of the pasts, because it will only make you stronger for your future.

I plan on taking 2020 by storm. With major prayer, patience and faith, I know God will guide me to the success he has that's meant solely for me.

Lastly, I'd like to thank everyone that stayed on my ass about continuing my writing. I love you guys so much. This may not be the book you expected, but it's the one that came from my heart. I have to be true to God, then myself.

Thank you,

Brittany Nicole!

Brittany Nicole's Catalogue:

Giving You My Love 1-2

She Wanna Be A Thug's Reality

Stay Connected with Brittany Nicole:

If you want to stay connected with me and find out how to get more sneak peeks, book conversations and just interacting with me:

IG: @authoressbrittanynicole

Amazon Author Page: Brittany Nicole

Author Group on FB: Brit's Urban Lit

Dear Diary

I'm so sick of not living the life that I deserve. I've been with the same man for five years and he's still not giving me the life I deserve. What woman in their right mind wants to be with a man that owns a janitorial company? Not this bitch! The best thing that's come from our relationship is my baby boy, but that's where it ends. Then, I have to watch this bitch get my dream man, my dream car, my dream everything. Why? Why didn't I get the life I deserve? What makes her so special that she gets the world and I'm left with her hand me downs. Before she became who she is now, I was That Bitch. Got to be fucking kidding me. This secondhand shit is about to end. I'm coming for everything that's meant for me. Even if it means taking something that doesn't belong to me. So be it.

Game on Bitch!

Signed, Jream Daniels… A Determined Bitch.

Jream Daniels

"Hmmm." Rolling my eyes upward, frustration was laced all over my face, but this nigga was none the wiser. You would think after years of me faking it while we have sex, he would have known by now. Looking at the clock and noticing its almost six in the morning was my only entertainment while he humped away in my vagina.

"Damn, baby, this pussy feels so fucking good," my boyfriend, Noah, said deeply in my ear. He has a very sexy, deep voice but no matter how sexy it is, I was completely turned off.

Noah and I have been together for five years and we share a three-year-old son together. I swear, Nyjae is the best thing that has ever happened to me, but his father and my relationship has finally run its course. He just didn't know it yet.

Feeling Noah pump harder inside of me, I knew that meant he was closing to cumming. Once again, he couldn't last longer than three funky ass minutes. It seemed like over the last couple years, our sex life had taken a deep plunge. Before Noah started his own janitorial business, he was working for this previous company. He would come home and deep stroke me all night long. Now that he has his own business that he's been trying to get off the ground for what's seems like the longest time, he can only give me three-minute dick.

"Ahh, baby! Shit. That was fucking amazing." Pushing Noah off me, I got up to go clean myself off and then go get my baby up for daycare.

"What's wrong with you, Jream?" Noah asked, standing in the doorway.

"Nothing at all. Can you please get out? I have to go get Nyjae up and ready for school." He looked at me like I hurt his feelings. Noah was a very handsome man. He just didn't do it for me anymore. If I'm being honest, he hasn't done it for me in a while. Don't get me wrong. His looks never changed. He was still that fine ass nigga I met five years ago. The only difference is, he stopped being the man that gave me everything my heart desired.

When I first met Noah, he was tall, dark and handsome. I had been out at a restaurant with my best friend, Lauriel and her sister, Taniece. Taniece had been the one to notice him first, and even said she was going to go speak to him. When she pointed him out, at first glance, I really thought I was looking at the actor Lance Gross; same height, build and skin complexion. He was so fucking sexy to me. So, I decided right then and there she didn't need a man that damn fine. I casually got my sexy ass up and did my sexiest walk towards him with no regard for my best friend's sister. I didn't care, the bitch didn't like me anyway. From the moment we met, he swept me off my feet and damn near gave me the world.

For the longest, you couldn't tell me that I hadn't hit the jack pot with my man. He was thirty years old, had a good job, no kids and catered to my every want and need. At the time, I was twenty-five and ready for a good man to take care of me. I wasn't anything like my best friend Lauriel. While my parents cut me off because I didn't want to go to school and get an education, Lauriel went to college. She had graduated from Southern University with a major in Fashion Design and a minor in Business. She fell in love with designing shoes and started her business.

That was not my life. I wanted to be a kept bitch and I planned on being just that. My money was starting to run low and Lauriel had offered me a job as her assistant until I could figure out something I wanted to do. I was insulted that she even thought I would take the job. Instead of taking the job, I offered for her to pay my bills until I figured something out. She thought I had lost my mind. Well, shit, I thought she wanted to help. Not long after, I met Noah.

Fast forward two years after we met. I had given birth to our son NyJae and Noah decided to venture off and start his own business. I was all for it until I realized the money he used to spend on me had to go towards his business. There were little to no vacations, no more shopping sprees, no more just because gifts, and worse of all, no more great dick. All he kept telling me was, *"Be patient, Jream. Your man will give you everything you deserve."* I didn't want to be patient. I never had to ask my parents twice, and now that I've been cut off by them. I had a man that said he wanted to take care of me. I shouldn't have to ask my man twice either.

Now I was thirty and he was thirty-five. He always came home so tired and broke. I was tired of the bullshit. Shit didn't seem like it was getting any better over the last three years. We were still in the same two-bedroom apartment that we got years ago. I was still riding around in the 2017 Benz he bought me a couple years ago, and I hadn't been shopping in God's knows how long. Every dollar he spends is on bills, food and our son. What the fuck about me?

"Baby, are you really going to act like this so early in the morning?" He tried to come and wrap his around me, but I pushed him back and slammed the bathroom door. He didn't deserve to touch me. This relationship had long ago run its course, but I'm not a dumb bitch. I know better than to leave one situation without securing another one.

After getting myself cleaned up, I look in the mirror, admiring my beauty. In my opinion, I was a bad bitch. I had the prettiest vanilla latte complexion and pearly white teeth. Standing at five foot six, I was still carrying a little bit of baby weight in all the right places. My breasts were a forty double-d. I had a flat tummy and a round ass that

Noah loved to grab on. Lauriel was always telling me that I needed to have more to offer a man besides my looks. I'd been doing just fine all this time. I didn't need her advice.

After I got dressed, I headed in the direction of my son's room, and I noticed Noah had already gotten him dressed. Completely ignoring Noah, I went over to my son and gave him a kiss on the forehead.

"Good morning, baby."

"Good morning, mommy." Gathering his things, I got him together to walk out of the door.

"Really, Jream? You're just going to leave without saying shit to me?" Noah asked with his uniform on, preparing to go to work.

"Bye, Noah." Leaving out of the door, I walked to my car and strapped Nyjae in his car seat.

His daycare was about twenty minutes away, so I decided to call Lauriel on the way.

"Lauriel Mathers speaking," she said in her professional voice.

"Bitch, don't act like you ain't know this was me calling you."

Laughing, she said, "Girl, I didn't even look at it before I answered. I just got to my office. I've been so busy working on my new line." Rolling my eyes upward, I didn't have time to hear about her shoes she made that she thought was hot.

"Oh well, I'm headed to drop of Nyjae to daycare," I said, completely changing the subject.

"Kiss my god baby for me. Jream, let me call you right back. Karter is calling me. I was supposed to call him as soon as I got to work this morning."

Smacking my lips in annoyance, "Once again, I have to hear about this Karter person and I don't know who he is. Is he even real?" I asked, laughing at my own joke.

"Yes, Bitch. My man is real. You're going to meet him real soon. Now bye!" She said, hanging up abruptly.

Shaking my head, I thought about the friendship between me and Lauriel. Sometimes I loved her and there were also times I hated her. Lauriel and I had been friends since we were fifteen, meeting at Warren Easton high school in New Orleans. She and I were from two totally different worlds. Lauriel and her sister, Taniece, lived in a lower-class community with their mother. Their father had left them years before I ever met her. While they lived in a single parent home, I lived in a two-parent home. My mother and father were very well accomplished, both being lawyers. From an early age, all I could remember was my parents giving me every single thing I wanted. There wasn't anything I didn't have at my fingertips.

Even with us being two completely different people, we kind of gravitated to one another. Part of me enjoyed having a friend that I felt like would always be jealous of the fact that I would have everything she couldn't have. The only problem was, Lauriel was nothing like that. When I got something handed to me by my parents, she would go out and work for it. While I graduated by the skin of my teeth, she graduated valedictorian and had numerous scholarships to any school she wanted to choose from. Needless to say, I was in a silent competition with Lauriel. The crazy thing is, she didn't even realize it. Her sister saw it. That's why the bitch hated me but I could care less. She could suck out my ass for all I care.

Any who, right now, I felt like I was winning. Yes, she

has her own business, but I have a handsome little boy. And even though I don't want him, I have a man that makes sure I don't have to lift a finger. I doubt her man is better than mines. I can't wait to meet her new man so I can continue rubbing in her face how I'm winning. Even when I find a new man and I drop Noah's limp dick ass, I'll still be winning.

Lauriel Mathers

"Taniece, can you please call the distributor and make sure they have all the fabrics I need for the designs I have laid out in this folder? Also, I need you to call different venues and find out the best prices for the launch party for my fall line," I said to my sister.

"No problem. You need to call Karter back. He just called me looking for you."

Sighing in frustration, "Shit, I forgot to call him again. I was too busy on the phone with Jream." As soon as those words left my lips, my sister rolled her eyes.

"I don't know why you're still wasting your time being friends with that hoe."

For the longest, Taniece had a dislike for Jream. She could never really explain why, but she never let me hear the end of how she truly felt about her. It became even worst when Jream decided to step to Noah even after Taniece said she was going to talk to him. I got in her ass about that too. I don't play about my sister, but I also had to take into consideration that man didn't even know

Taniece.

"Anyway, can you please go do what I asked you to while I call my man back," I said and stuck my tongue out at my sister.

She rolled her eyes and walked out. Taniece had been my assistant since her third year in college. She was at school on a scholarship and funds were low. She worked on campus but as soon as I had the funds to hire my sister, I did. I wanted her to have the money she needed for anything she needed it for. I offered the job to Jream first. Her parents had just cut her off because they were tired of footing the bill for her and she had no intentions on doing anything with her life. She declined and basically looked at me like I had shit on my face because I offered her a job.

At the age of twenty-five, I had started my shoe design business, Glamour Shoes. Growing up, I always had this thing for shoes. My mother didn't have the money to keep buying my sister and I new shoes, so I would recreate my own. If I had an old pair of white shoes, I'd clean them as best as I could and put my own personal designs on them. So, when I got to college, there wasn't anything else I wanted to major in but fashion design and business. I worked my ass off to save money to open my business, and thankfully, with a loan from the bank, I was able to make it happen.

So, here I am five years later, thirty years old and creating shoes for everyone, including some local New Orleans stars. I designed shoes for men and women. Most recently, I was contacted by the assistant of Karter Montegue, wide receiver for the New Orleans Saints. He was the second highest paid receiver in the NFL. He was hosting a charity fundraiser and he wanted some shoes that no one could buy off the shelf.

After going over the details with his team, I never imagined the day of the event he would actually come to my show room and pick up his shoes. Baby, I tell you when this man walked into the room, It felt like my entire world stopped. Now, don't get me wrong, I'm a Saints fan, but I watch the sport. I don't get all into the players and names. The only person I really know is the quarterback.

Karter strutted in the room wearing a simply fitted, blue, crew neck t-shirt. He had on some slightly baggy blue jeans and some black and blue Jordan's gracing his feet. Around his neck was a small gold chain. His face was one I had etched in my memory from our first encounter. His deep, caramel complexion, chocolate brown eyes and a sexy goatee that highlighted his gorgeous smile enticed my soul. He liked to keep his hair cut in a faded Caesar and it looked damn good on him.

From the moment he stepped foot in the door, let's just say he enjoyed the sight before him just as much as I did. I wasn't insecure about my looks, but I didn't think I had what it took to get an NFL player. I had skin like Hershey dark chocolate. I had a slim frame that looked good with my five-five height. The only curve I had on my body was my butt because my breasts weren't much to write home about. The most unique thing on me was the greyish green eyes I inherited from my mother.

Needless to say, after I gave him his shoes, we exchanged numbers and had been joined at the hip ever since. That was about three months ago and as more time passed, the more serious we became. The only person Karter had met so far was my sister. She adored him. They had already formed their own "in-law" relationship. I wasn't ready for him to meet my mother and my crazy ass auntie, nor was I ready for him to meet my best friend. I wasn't ready for her snide remarks nor her scrutiny. Of course, I had told her about him, but that was it. I didn't give her a last name, nor did I even send a picture. I loved Jream, I really did, but she had a tendency to try and make everything about her. And when it wasn't, everything went wrong.

For years, I've dealt with that side of her and had just accepted her as she was, but I wasn't ready to expose that to Karter. I was falling deeply in love with him and I wanted to keep us away from the bullshit as long as I could.

Finally getting my head on straight, I pick up the phone to call my man.

"Damn, bae, you're just finding time to call me?" Karter said, out of breath.

Looking at the time, I noticed it was damn near eleven in the morning. I knew he did his morning workout around this time. With it being the off season, he liked to keep his mind and body in shape. I really let the time escape me.

"I'm sorry, baby. As soon as I got to work, I started working on the designs for the new line and I had Taniece making a bunch of phone calls."

"It's alright, baby, I just like to know you made it their safely. You gon' have me either staying at your house and bringing you to work or meeting you there in the morning so I'll know you made it safely. I shouldn't have to call Taniece to check on you." I heard the frustration in his voice. Because we've only been dating for three months, we still live separately. We haven't gone public with our relationship and that's just how I like it. There's no one in our business. I can spend as much time as I want at his house or he's at mines. Nobody knows but us.

"I understand. How about you meet me at my house when I leave here tonight and it can just be us tonight? I know I've been really busy lately and you've been very understanding. I love you for that." I froze as soon as the words left my lips. Although I knew I was falling for Karter, neither of us had expressed it.

"What did you say, baby?" He said and I heard the smile in his voice.

"Ugh! I ain't say nothing." I refused to repeat myself.

"Nah, keep that same energy you had a minute ago. You said you love a nigga."

"You really make me sick." I couldn't help but laugh, but my stomach was still in knots after what I had just accidently said.

"I don't care how sick I make you. You just said you love me. My baby love me! Well, I'm a happy ass man because I love you too, baby."

"Lauriel, the distributor is on line two. He said he needs to talk to you about one of the fabrics you requested," my sister said over the intercom.

Before I could say anything, Karter said, "That's cool, bae, I heard T. Go handle your business and have that ass ready for tonight. Love you, mama!" Without waiting for a reply, he hung up.

Wishing I could bask in the fact that my man expressed his love to me, I had to put that to side for a little while and get back to business.

*

"I'm about to head out, sis. Do you need anything

before I leave?" I asked Taniece before I walked out the door.

"No. I'm good actually. Text me to let me know you made it safely."

"Taniece, don't stay here too late. It's already eight o'clock."

Smacking her lips, my sister said, "Good night, Lauriel. I only have to send out these emails to the vendors about pricing for the launch party. Just trying to get a head start on tomorrow."

Shaking my head, I told her goodnight and walked out of my showroom. I can honestly say, hiring my sister was the best decision I could have made. She knows how important my business was to me, so she treated it like it was her own. She was still in school working on her master's in human resources. If my business continues to flourish like I plan for it to, by the time she graduates, I can make her head of Human Resources and we can run my business together.

Locking the door behind me and making my way to my Matte Black 2019 Audi, I got in my car, ready to head home for the night. I was hoping Karter remembered to meet me at my house tonight. I wasn't too worried because he was really good at keeping his word. Getting on the interstate to take the twenty-minute ride from New Orleans to Harrahan, I let the radio be my company on the ride home.

"I finally found the nerve to say, I'm gonna make a change in my life, it's starting here today. I surrender all my love, I never thought I could. I'm giving all my love away and it's only one reason that I would. Baby it's You!"

Listening to *You* by Jesse Powell bought a bright smile to my face. It made me think about Karter.

In the beginning of our relationship, I told myself I was crazy to be involving myself with an NFL athlete. I've heard the reputations of some of those guys and I refused to have that life for myself. I took relationships serious. Which is why I hadn't been in one since my sophomore year of college. The last guy I dated didn't believe in being faithful, so I let him go be a hoe without involving me. I just had friends here and there over the years. A consistent person to scratch that itch every now and again. Nothing serious. But Karter made me want to be serious with him. His personality was so inviting and his ambition made me want to push harder. I couldn't wait until the new football season started so I could be his biggest cheerleader.

Finally pulling up to my two-level townhouse, I saw his Aston Martin in my driveway. I get excited just thinking about seeing him. Walking up to his car, I expect to see him sitting inside waiting on me, but I was shocked to find it empty.

Pulling my key out to go unlock my door, I got the surprise of my life. Candles were lit all over my living room with a trail of rose pedals starting from my door to the stairs. Seeing a note taped to my banister, I read it.

"I know you're wondering how I got inside. Worry about that later. A hot bubble bath is waiting for you right now. Get your sexy ass upstairs and get naked. Enjoy, baby."

I started laughing because he knew me so well. I was wondering how he got in my house, but I'm pretty sure it had everything to do with my sister. She was my biggest supporter, so anytime someone wanted to do anything nice for me, she was their biggest help.

Taking my four-inch pumps off at the door, I made my way upstairs to see what was waiting for me. Walking in my room, I saw more rose pedals leading up to my bathroom. Going inside, my jacuzzi tub was filled to the rim with bubbles, and there was a tray on the side with a glass of my favorite wine, Pinot Noir Meiomi. Shedding my clothes, I got in the tub and the hot water relaxed my muscles. I allowed my body to enjoy the water for about thirty minutes before I got anxious and decided to get out and look for Karter.

I pinned my hair up in a bun on top of my head and wrapped a towel around my body. I walk out of the bathroom and there he was. Standing next to my bed, shirtless, wearing only a pair of silk boxers. Looking at his chiseled chest and him staring at me with that gorgeous smile made my juices flow.

"Hey, baby. Did you enjoy your bath?" He asked in his deep baritone voice.

"Yeah, I did. Thank you for the surprise, baby."

"Oh no, the night is only beginning. Come here." He

looked at me, motioning his finger for me to come forward.

Karter grabbed my hand and pulled me gently to him. He pecked me on the lips before motioning for me to lay down on my stomach. He unwrapped my towel and laid it across my ass. Slowly, he rubbed my back with what felt like warm oil. My eyes fluttered in the back of my head because his hands felt so good on my skin. Surprisingly, his hands weren't terribly rough from using them so much. They had a softness to them that were just right for what he's doing to me.

After spending a good ten minutes kneading my back and shoulders, he moved his hands down to my ass and began rubbing it in a circular motion. It felt so damn good that all I could do was moan in appreciation.

"You like that, bae?" He asked.

"Yes, baby. It feels good."

"What about this?" Opening my ass cheeks, he used his thumb to glide up and down from my ass crack to my vagina. Because it made me hornier, my hips involuntarily rose upward to give him better access to the main goal. Instead of continuing his assault on my body with his fingers, he replaced his thumb with his tongue.

"Aww shit," I couldn't help saying in that moment. Feeling Karter eat me out from the back was making me go crazy. We've had sex before, but it seems like each time we do it, it gets better and better.

"Ummm umm." Hearing him moan in my pussy made me wetter. Instead of staying on my stomach, he turned me over on my back and dove head first back in. He took my hand and put it on the back of his head. I couldn't help but to push him deeper in my pussy so he can taste every drop that I was about to give him.

"Ohhh, Karter. I'm cumming. You're making me come, baby!" Grinding my womanhood all over his face to receive the orgasm I so desperately needed, I knew I would be coming within seconds.

Looking up at me with a devilish grin, I saw my juices dripping down his goatee. Not having any words in me, I raise up on the bed and pulled his boxers down his body. Neither of us said a word as I admired all nine inches of his girth. Karter had the biggest dick that I've ever encountered and he left me speechless after every session we shared.

I was salivating in anticipation of having him in my mouth. During the three months we've been together, I have never gone down on him. Well, all that changes tonight. After the way his tongue had me damn near climbing the walls, he deserved every bit of this throat. I grabbed his dick in my hands and slid my tongue over the head. His cleanliness was impressive. Instead of teasing him the way I wanted to, my nasty ass couldn't handle that, so I just swallowed him whole.

"What the fuck, Lauriel? The fuck you doing?" He said as he grabbed the back of my head.

I didn't need any directions as I glided him in and out of my mouth. Making my mouth so wet, I had spit damn near falling out of it. His sexy ass tasted so good. I didn't give a fuck about how freaky I was getting. Taking him all the way to the back of my throat, I relaxed my muscles and extended my tongue out to lick his nuts.

"Nah, fuck this. Your ass not about to have me coming in two minutes. Lay your ass back and open them legs," he said, pulling himself out of my mouth. I couldn't help but to laugh at his statement. Preparing myself for him to fuck me in submission, I laid back like he told me to. Karter climbed on the bed and positioned his self between my legs.

"Don't think we're not gonna talk about the shit you just pulled. Shit got my head fucked up." He's going to be surprised to find out I watched pornos to learn what I just did.

Finally pushing his manhood inside me, it filled me up to capacity.

"How the fuck this pussy so tight? I'll never understand it," he basically whispered to himself.

Wrapping my legs around his back, he groaned deeply then kissed me passionately.

"Baby, you feel so good inside me." Normally after a few strokes, we'd be having rough passionate sex. Not tonight. Tonight, he was taking his time with me. Staring me deeply in my eyes and watching what his strokes were doing to me.

"You feel so fucking good, girl. You got a nigga ready to bust and we just started." He started working his hips in a circular motion. The friction from his movements were hitting my g-spot.

"Karter, bae, don't stop. Right there, baby." I was so close to cumming. He took my left leg and threw it over his left shoulder. He lifted my hips just a little and started giving me short, hard strokes that had me cumming in ten seconds flat.

"Come on, baby, I feel my pussy tightening on my dick. Let that shit go. Come with me, baby." I was lost for words. Right after he said that, he kissed me so hard, it felt like he was breathing for me. We were cumming in unison.

"Got damn, girl. That was the most intense shit I've ever experienced in my life," Karter said while breathing hard.

"Me too, baby." He climbed off me, laid on his back and pulled me close. He kissed me gently on the forehead.

"I love your ass, Lauriel Mathers. I know we only been at this shit for a few months but I know how I feel."

"I love you too, Karter Montegue."

"I'm glad the feeling is mutual, baby," he said while holding me tight.

For the rest of the night, we stayed cuddled in each other's arms talking about his future, my future and our future. When my morning started, I didn't know it was going to start with my blurting out that I loved Karter. I didn't think he was ready for me to express such sentiment to him, so I was prepared to sit on it until I felt like he was ready to hear it. Boy, did he prove me wrong. Now, it was just time to decide when we planned to share our love with the rest of the world.

Taniece Mathers

Walking inside of my apartment, I noticed it was ten o'clock at night. I was exhausted after staying a couple hours more than usual at the showroom. I won't complain because I enjoyed working for my sister. The pay was good, and the experience was even better. She didn't make the work environment unbearable, but she didn't play about making her business look bad either.

Heading in my bathroom to turn on the shower, I was stopped by my ringing cellphone. *Noah? Why is he calling me?*

"Hello?" I answered in surprise.

"Hey, Taniece. I'm sorry to be calling you so late, but I honestly didn't know who else to call. I tried calling Lauriel but she didn't answer and you were my only other hope."

"Uh, yea. Are you okay?" I asked in confusion.

"Yea, I'm ok. I guess...Well, not really." He paused for a second. "Shit, I honestly don't know." Now, I was even more confused.

"Noah, what's going on? Is Nyjae ok?" Even though I couldn't stand his hoe of a mother, I loved that little boy as if he was my own. He was my stanka and I was his Tee Niece.

"Yea. Nyjae is fine. I'm sorry I'm making you worry. The reason I'm calling is because of Jream." I swear, every time I heard that bitch's name, I rolled my damn eyes. I had to be careful before they get stuck like that.

"What about Jream?"

"Have you spoken to her lately? I don't know what's going on with her. It's like she hates me. She barely says two words to me, and she doesn't even let me touch her." Poor Noah. He sounded really frustrated.

"Well, in all honesty, I haven't spoken to her in while." Of course, I never spoke to the bitch. That was my sister's so-called best friend, not mines.

He sighed deeply. "Fuck. I had to try. I knew if anybody knew what was going on with her, it would be you or Lauriel. You guys are her best friends. I would have tried her parents but I know they don't have much to do with Jream." My eyes almost popped out of my head at the mention of me being one of Jream's best friends. I know that bitch didn't say that so he had to assume it.

Instead of saying what I wanted to out loud, I only gave him words of encouragement.

"I'm sorry, Noah. I wish I could help you. I honestly haven't talked to Jream in a while, but I'm sure it's nothing. You know us women have monthly mood swings."

"Yeah, maybe you're right. I just know with money being so tight over the last few years, and feeling like we're drifting apart, I didn't know if she had mentioned something to you guys. A nigga just stressed." He took another pause and said, "You know what, I'm sorry I even bothered you with all this. Have a good night, T." With that, he abruptly ended the call.

He didn't know it, but he gave me an earful and a mouthful. Poor Noah. He didn't know it but if money was so tight, that's why Jream wasn't being the perfect little housewife anymore. That hoe was money hungry.

I know it may seem like I had an extreme hate for Jream, but it wasn't always like that. She was actually really cool when my sister and I first met her. I was five years younger than them so when I met her at ten years old, I was too young to see her for who she really was. Over the years, I started to notice how she was in competition with my sister. While Lauriel would be her biggest cheerleader, Jream would be Lauriel's biggest hater. I never understood how my sister wouldn't catch on to her hating ass comments.

For instance, when a boy would approach my sister that Jream thought was cute, she'd encourage Lauriel to deny his advances. Or if her parents bought something for her, she would flaunt in our faces. Stuff like that never mattered to us. If we wanted something, we'd go out and work for it. It never bothered us that our mother couldn't afford anything other than rent, bills and the essential items.

When Lauriel was graduating from getting her Master's in Business, Jream's parents were cutting her off for sitting on her ass. She was pissed at my sister for offering her a job and not just giving her the money she needed for her bills. They think I don't know that tidbit of information, but my nosey ass heard the argument. Jream basically told my sister she wasn't a real friend because she didn't want to help her. Lauriel told her she was helping her by trying to give her a job. Well, Miss Jream said working for a friend was beneath her. Baby, my goose was cooked. I couldn't believe that bitch's audacity. I already didn't like the hoe, but that made me dislike her even more. What kind of real woman would want another woman footing her bills? Especially one she wasn't fucking. Jream Daniels was that kind of bitch.

After a few weeks of them not speaking, they finally made up. For the first time in my life, I looked at my sister like she was a dumb bitch for even entertaining that slut bucket. But she told me that was still her best friend and she loved Jream for reasons I wouldn't understand. That was the moment I decided to keep my comments to myself and let my sister learn the hard way. I'm lying, I still told her I didn't like the bitch. But I kept everything else to myself.

What really closed the door of any kind of relationship I could have ever had with Jream was the night I spotted Noah across the restaurant. I never believed in love at first sight until that very night. I remember some girls in school talking about when they met their first love, everything else in the room stopped. Well, that's how I felt the night I saw Noah. At that time, I was only twenty years old, in my second year in college and still a virgin. Even though I was a virgin, I didn't hold back how I felt. If I was interested in you, I let you know. I made the worst mistake ever that night when I told Lauriel and Jream that I saw Noah chilling at the bar. His handsome ass was none the wiser to the dirty ass thoughts running through my mind. When I expressed interest and prepared myself to go speak to him, Jream had already beat me to it. Needless to say, I was beyond pissed. I know I didn't know the nigga but damn. I opened my mouth and said I was going to go speak to him.

That bitch didn't care. She was so secure in her looks that she walked her light bright ass right over to him and sank her claws into him. I was just as secure in myself. I actually looked exactly like my sister, except my breast were a little bit bigger. I was ready for him to experience all this chocolate, but she snatched his fine ass up and made him her man in no time. For the past five years, I've watched him be a damn good man to that girl and she was so ungrateful. When she got pregnant, I had decided to put my feelings aside because it seemed like they were really in love. Then, Noah decided to follow his dream and open his own business. Jream's true colors came flying back out. All she talked about was how broke he was, how he couldn't buy her the latest hand bag anymore, or how he couldn't upgrade her car.

The bitch was insane. Do you know how many women, good women, would love to be with a man that had the ambition to own their own shit? I know I did. Thugging it out for a few tough years didn't compare to the return it would bring if his business started turning a profit. I knew that Noah would make it happen. He was smart and had the drive. He just needed the woman he was with to have his back. Sadly, I knew Jream wasn't it. But no matter how I felt, I would never throw salt on her game. That wasn't the type of bitch my mother raised me to be.

It also didn't make it any better that he and I had a friendship. Like tonight, he felt comfortable calling me when something was on his mind. He never flirted with me or gave me an inkling that he even looked at me as anything other than his friend. Neither did I. I respected relationships and no matter how I felt about him, I would keep it to myself.

Still, here I am, twenty-five years old and still a virgin. I refused to give my pussy to an unworthy nigga. I didn't care how long I had to wait.

That night, in the restaurant, I thought Noah could have potentially been that mad but he didn't even know how I felt. I tried for years to suppress the feelings I had for him. My sister didn't even know. It was hard with him being in such close proximity and the fact I'm watching him be a good man to an undeserving woman. Noah, nor Nyjae deserved that. Don't get me wrong. Jream was a good mom, but only when it was convenient for her. There was many a day when she would call my sister to keep Nyjae because she needed a break. A break from what was my question. I truly understand full time moms have it hard, but this girl didn't work. Nyjae would be at daycare eight or nine hours out of the day and she was at home doing nothing.

No matter the fact, as long as she wasn't mistreating my stanka, she wouldn't have a problem with me. When it comes to Noah, if she knew what was good for her, she'd do better and take care of her man.

Jream

Today started just like any other day. Noah woke me up to give me some terrible dick and I got my son up and ready for daycare. Except today, I went to get my hair done. That was something I hadn't done in a long time because our funds were low. But today, I didn't care. I felt the need to splurge on myself. It felt so good to have my scalp massaged and scratched. I didn't care how much I had to spend, I just knew I deserved it. Afterwards, I went home to lounge around and wait to go pick up my baby.

In the middle of enjoying my day, Lauriel called me and invited me to lunch with her and Taniece. I really didn't feel like being bothered with Taniece, but for a free meal, I'd deal with it today. It had been a while since Lauriel and I had gotten together. She called herself being so busy with her little business, she didn't have time for me.

Pulling up in the parking lot of Olive Garden, I started to frown. She knows this is my least favorite place to eat but she chose it anyway. Walking inside, I didn't even bother to wait on the hostess to seat me, I walked directly to where I saw them sitting. I glided pass the other patrons wearing a red, spaghetti strapped tank top, some light-colored ripped jeans and my red stilettos. I'm hoping they were mesmerized by my luxurious, dark brown extensions that came down my back and stopped right above my ass.

I knew Noah would try to curse my ass out when he saw how much I spent, but I didn't give a damn. I needed to do something for myself and getting my hair done made me feel better.

"Hello, ladies. Girl, what made you pick this place? You know I can barely stand this place," I greeted them nicely even though I was getting the evil eye from Taniece.

"Well, you didn't have to come," Taniece said under her breath.

Trying to diffuse the situation, Lauriel said, "Hey, girl. You look beautiful. Did you just get your hair done?" Leave it to Lauriel to notice the little things.

"Yeah, girl. I just left from Tinky. You know she's the only one I let touch my hair."

Lauriel and I had been going to the same hairstylist for

years. When she moved into a shop, her prices went up. Up until Noah's pockets hit a snag, it had never been a problem spending however much I needed to get my hair right. Now Lauriel was looking at me funny.

"What, bitch?" I asked snidely.

"You went to Tinky? Didn't you tell me money was a little funny? You know I know how much she charges for that kind of style." I couldn't believe this bitch's audacity. Yea, she tried to whisper it, but to bring up my finances in public was some bullshit.

"I was able to get it done, wasn't I? Stop worrying about my money being funny and you worry about that fake ass man we have yet to meet." Her eyes bucked out of her head at my words.

"Fake? Girl, bye. My brother-in-law is not fake. Just because you haven't met him doesn't mean he's fake." Of course, Taniece would come to her sister's rescue.

"Have you met him?" I asked waiting for her to tell me no.

"Yeah. I've met him. Been around him a few times." That made my head jerk in the direction of Lauriel. This was news to me. I thought nobody had met him.

"So, Bestie, you holding out on me?" Before she could answer me, her phone started ringing.

"Hey, baby... Yea, I'm at Olive Garden by Esplanade with T and Jream... Yeah... ok, love you." Now that made me choke on my water.

"Love you??? We've gotten that close and I haven't met him."

She sighed deeply. "No, Jream, you haven't met him. Can I keep something to myself? Damn." I wanted to laugh so bad because it seemed like I was getting under her skin. I loved it.

"What's wrong with him? He ugly? Broke? Girl, you know I won't judge."

After I finished my sentence, I noticed Taniece smirking at me.

"What's funny?" I really wanted to know.

"Nothing. Nothing at all. I just can't wait for you to meet him." I saw Lauriel nudge her after her comment. I wondered what that was about, but I decided to leave it alone and focus of lunch.

Pulling out the menu to look it over, I noticed a commotion at the front of the restaurant.

"Awww shit, nah." I hear Taniece say in her messy ass voice. I didn't get it, so I didn't comment. I continued being nosey trying to see what all the commotion was about.

Before I could wonder any longer, I see that fine motherfucker, Karter Montegue. I wasn't a football fan whatsoever, but I knew who his ass was. This man was the finest nigga walking the earth. I saw him sign a few autographs then he started a big dick nigga strut further into the restaurant.

You know what a big dick nigga strut is. When you see them niggas walking like their trying to have room for that big ass dick that's swinging between their legs. Shit was sexy as fuck.

"Wait a minute. Is he coming over here?" Thank God, I got my hair done today. I knew it wasn't going to be long before I found my next nigga.

His fine ass walked up to our table and stood tall before the three of us.

"Hello, beautiful ladies." Then he looked towards me and extended his hand. I looked towards Lauriel and Taniece, hoping I saw a lick of jealousy. I saw none, but I knew better.

"How are you? You must be, Miss Jream. It's nice to put a face to a name." I was taken aback that he knew my name.

Before I could question it, he said, "Lauriel has told me so much about you."

Wait, what? Looking between him and Lauriel, I was speechless. In that moment, it was like a light bulb went off in my head. I looked towards Lauriel for clarification.

"Wait a minute. Karter? You're thee Karter?" I asked in shock.

He started to laugh, but I didn't find a motherfucking thing funny. This bitch never told me her new man was my dream man. My pussy had been aching just watching this fine ass specimen on tv. Something was fucking wrong with this picture.

"Yes, Ma'am. I'm thee Karter. Damn, baby, your friend seems surprised I'm that nigga."

Finally finding her voice, Lauriel said, "She is surprised. I never told her your last name. Only that your name was Karter." Her tone was really dry. Like she'd rather be any place but here. I didn't care about none of that. I wanted to know how this bitch pulled this shit off. She was dating a fucking multimillionaire, superstar athlete while I was with a fucking janitor. This shit was all wrong.

He walked over, pulled her out of her seat and held her tightly. He looked down at her attentively. The look of contentment on their faces was disgusting.

"You wanted to keep your man all to yourself?" She blushed then place her head on his chest. Ugh. This shit was sickening to watch. What did he see in her? Lauriel didn't have what it took to be with a man of his stature. He needed a woman like me on his arm. I couldn't believe this bullshit.

"Are you ok, Jream? Aren't you happy for your best friend?" Taniece asked me in a questioning tone. She was looking at me skeptically. I knew why, but I refuse to give her the satisfaction.

I put on my best smile and said, "Of course I am." I started gathering my things. It honestly hurt to fake my happiness.

"It was really nice meeting you, Karter. I have to go get my son from daycare." Before I could let them question why I was going get Nyjae from school at only twelve pm, I got the hell out of dodge.

*

Sitting on the sofa with a glass of wine, I hadn't been able to do much since I had gotten home from that bullshit ass lunch with Lauriel. Besides feeding my son and putting him down to sleep, I hadn't moved from this spot. My mind was boggled. I honestly couldn't believe she was able to snag such an eligible bachelor.

Karter Montegue was one of the most successful players in the league. His net worth was in the millions and vastly rising. He was the perfect candidate to secure so I could leave Noah's broke ass behind. I had no clue how Lauriel pulled this shit, but I had to put a stop to it. He was not the man for her. Don't get me wrong, Lauriel was a good girl, but she wasn't of my caliber. Yes, she went to college and owned her own business, but a man like that didn't want an independent woman. He wanted a woman that would be at his every beck and call. I was just the woman he needed. I don't know how I was going to pull it off, but he had to see that I was the woman he needed.

Lauriel knew the life of a professional woman, not of a socialite. She was never of the upper class. She didn't know how to conduct herself in such settings. Lauriel wouldn't know what to do at those fundraiser functions and team gatherings. Knowing all this gave me the upper hand on how to approach this situation. Shit, I don't care if I had to get grimy and dirty, I was gonna get my man.

I was getting excited just thinking about how I was going to get this man for myself. Yes, I knew it would hurt Lauriel, but she was strong. She would get over it. Besides, she needed to find a man that was more her speed. Karter Montegue was not it.

Hearing keys jiggle in the locks, I prepared myself to deal with Noah's ass another night. I couldn't wait until I rid myself of his ass.

"Twelve hundred dollars, Jream?" I heard him yell

from the door.

"What?" I look at him like he's crazy.

"You spend twelve hundred dollars on getting your hair done? You do know that was our rent money, right?"

I looked at him like I could care less. "Ok, what is that supposed to mean to me? I needed my hair done." In all the years that we had been together, Noah had never so much as put his foot down with me. His mission in life was to make me happy and he'd been fucking that up for a while.

"Jream, you're jeopardizing having a place to lay our heads for you to get your head done? How fucking selfish is that?" I knew he was mad. If he was a lighter skin man, he would be turning red. It was amusing though. He was so pissed, the vein in his neck was sticking out.

"Well, I suggest you go figure it out. Matter fact, you need to start figuring out a lot. I didn't sign up for this shit. When I met you, you had endless amount of funds, now I'm getting pennies. This shit isn't worth it."

As soon as the words left my mouth, I knew I had to calm down. I wasn't in the position to be making many demands. If I still had my parents in my back pocket, I would have left a long time ago. Hell, if I knew Lauriel wouldn't have minded helping me out, I would have gotten ghost then. I was moving too fast too soon.

It was just the fact that I knew I planned on making Karter my man made me anxious to be rid of this broke ass nigga. He didn't even deserve to smell my pussy again. But I was willing to hand it to Karter on a silver platter. Despite the aggravation written all over my face, Noah walked towards me and grabbed my hands.

"Jream, baby, I know things are tight, but I promise, if you give me six more months, things will be better. I haven't been working this hard for nothing."

I could hear the sincerity in his voice but it did nothing for me. It was already too late. We would have never had this problem if nothing had changed. If Noah had kept his last job and not followed this pipe dream, we would have been fine. He knew he didn't have the money to have a business and keep me in his corner before he decided to do this. It was bad enough I stuck around for the last three years. I was just tired now. A bitch could do bad all by herself. I still wasn't stupid. I was going to tread lightly until I snagged the big fish.

So instead of expressing that sentiment, I lied. "I'm sorry, baby. I should have been more careful with our money. I'll do better." I almost wanted to laugh in his face. The look he gave me let me know he believed me. It's sad that after all these years, this nigga didn't know me at all. He actually thought I loved him. Truth is, I had love for Noah. He was my son's father and we had been through a lot together. But love didn't do anything for me. Money was what I needed. Money was what my son needed. We couldn't live off love.

Seeming to be buying my bullshit, he said, "Thank you, baby. Come on, let's go to bed." He hugged me tight and pulled me towards the bedroom. I knew I had to prepare myself for the three-minute dick I was about to receive. Only tonight, I had that fine ass Karter Montegue to entertain my thoughts instead the clock on the wall.

Lauriel

Today was finally the day I was going to showcase my new line at my launch party. Since this was my fifth year in business, I decided to do it big. My sister was able to acquire the W Hotel in New Orleans to give us an amazing discount to use their ballroom. I had the best event planners and caterers for the night. Besides having my fall line on display for all to see, I also reached out to a few local celebs and social media influencers like Supa and Inayah Lamis. Taniece was even able to snag Toya Wright. She got all their sizes to create each person a shoe specially made for them. My sister came up with the brilliant idea to pick six people to create a specific shoe for each and they can flaunt it on our special blue carpet. They would be like our moving artwork. I also had to honor Nipsey Hussle with a blue carpet instead of a red one.

Tonight is also the night Karter will get to meet my mother and some of my family. We sat down and talked about going public with our relationship and he assured me that everything would be ok. Granted, I was a little scared because he was so deep in the public eye while I was still working my ass off to make a name for myself in the fashion world. I didn't want anything to jeopardize that.

"Damn, baby. You look beautiful." I blushed from his compliment. Tonight was a special night for me. I wanted the event to be dressy casual. I wanted everyone that attended to enjoy themselves and be comfortable.

I was wearing my royal blue Round and Round You Go Dress by Fashion Nova. It was a beautiful off the shoulder dress that showed off my small cleavage and had a sexy split that started from the middle of my thighs and flared out to the floor. I paired my dress with my gold spiked red bottoms. I worked so hard to design shoes for everyone else, I didn't have the time to make my own damn shoes. I had my natural tresses flowing down my back in soft curls and my sister had found this really dope makeup artist on Instagram named R_0fficial. She had my face beat to the Gods. I looked and felt beautiful.

"Thank you, baby. You look damn good yourself." My handsome ass man was staring back at me in a royal blue suede suit jacket with a black dress shirt underneath and black pants. On his feet were some custom-made, black, diamond studded loafers that I made specifically for him. He was wearing his simple good chain that I loved. His cologne smelled so good. I couldn't wait to get back home so I could rip that suit off him.

"I see that look in your eyes and as bad as I want to bend your sexy ass over, we need to go," he said with a laugh.

"You're right, baby. Let me get my clutch and I'll be ready."

Gathering everything I needed to head out the door, we made our way outside and to my surprise, there was a shiny black Phantom waiting for us.

"Karter, really?" I looked at him in shock.

"Tonight is a special night for you, baby. I wanted it to be a night you wouldn't forget."

I leaned forward to kiss him passionately. Karter was really a dream come true. If there was any time I would doubt our relationship, he did something to make me ignore those feelings.

Getting in the back of the car, we made our way to the

Hotel. Making it there after about twenty-five minutes, we pulled up to the venue. Getting out and making it inside, the sight before me was so beautiful. Right outside of the ballroom, they had the blue carpet set up and a back drop of my logo on the wall. There were at least fifteen photographers there taking pictures. My sister had managed to get the local news stations and even a few Instagram blog sites on the blue carpet.

Karter grabbed my hand because this was our moment to let the world know we were together. He stood behind me and wrapped his arms around me to pose for pictures.

"Hi Everybody, this is Staria from All Tea, All Day and we are here with the beautiful Lauriel Mathers. Owner and Proprietor of Glamour Shoes." As soon as she spoke, I knew exactly who she was. Staria was a very well-known blogger from Instagram. With over three million followers, her site made a huge impact on social media. I don't know how Taniece pulled this off, but she deserved a raise.

"Hi, Staria. How are you tonight?"

"I'm doing quite well, but I have to say congratulations on all your success. Your assistant allowed us to have a secret walk through and I must say, your shoes are amazing," she complimented.

"Thank you so much. That means a lot coming from you."

She began to ask me what made me want to design shoes. I loved when I was asked that question. Explaining to people the joy I felt when I created something from nothing that people would love was everything to me. Most people were plagued with going to a nine to five they hated every day. I was blessed to make my own hours and create my own dreams. Staria once again wished me a congratulations and I thanked her again.

"You're welcome, gorgeous," she said then looked at Karter. "While I'm extending my congrats, you know it wouldn't be me if I didn't get all the tea." She winked at me slyly. "What do we have here? You and Mr. Karter Montegue," she said with a smile.

I looked up at Karter. He winked at me and flashed that handsome smile at me.

"Yes, Ms. Staria. I'm here to support my lady tonight." I blushed after he said that.

"Your lady? Are you guys telling the world that you are a couple?" Of course, Staria wouldn't leave until she got a full admission of the truth.

We both started laughing. Instead of coming straight out with an answer, Karter leaned down and kissed me softly on the lips.

"Does that give you your answer?" Karter asked in his sexy deep voice.

"Yes, sir, it does. Well there you have it, folks. Owner of Glamour Shoes, Lauriel Mathers and star wide receiver of the New Orleans Saints, Karter Montegue, have just let the world know they are a couple. And they are a beautiful couple, if I may add."

After thanking her for an amazing interview, we finally made our way inside of the ballroom.

The sight before me nearly moved me to tears. Each shoe for the new fall line had a beautiful display. The color scheme for the night was Royal Blue, Gold and Ivory. The tables were decorated beautifully with decorative shoe center pieces. I was amazed at the décor. The invitations had instructions for all the guests to wear all white. It was beautiful to see everybody followed directions. Looking around the room, I saw my mother, my aunts and my cousins sitting at the table designated for them.

Noticing the direction I was looking in, Karter said, "Come on, baby. I'm ready to meet your people."

"I want that same energy when it's time to meet your people." He started laughing.

I know how ghetto my family can get so I was dreading this meet and greet. See, Karter wasn't from here. He was from Cleveland and played football from Ohio State. He was determined to get his education so he stayed all four years, then was drafted to the Saints right after graduation. At twenty-eight, he's been in New Orleans for the last six years. He didn't know much about these crazy Louisiana people.

Walking up to my family's table, I went to speak to my mother.

"Hey, mama." Turning to greet me, my beautiful mother graced me with a smile.

Vera Mathers was the most beautiful woman in the world to me. She passed down her looks and that same chocolate skin to me and my sister. At the age of fifty, my mother still looked like she could pass for my age. She ate healthy and exercised daily. People often believed that we were sisters.

"Hey, baby! I'm so proud of you, Lauriel. Everything looks so beautiful." Her words meant a lot to me. Making my mother proud was important to me. She had worked so hard to give Taniece and I everything we needed. I just wanted to be able to take care of her the same or better.

"Thank you, Mama. Have you seen T anywhere?"

"That girl is running around here like a chicken with her head cut off. She's ok." Looking behind me towards Karter, she said, "Who is this handsome gentleman holding your hand?"

"How are you, ma'am? I'm Karter Montegue," he replied, reaching his hand out towards my mother.

"FINE ASS KARTER MONTEGUE? THE FOOTBALL PLAYER?" My loud ass auntie Tina said. She hates her government name. She prefers everyone call her Teeny Boo.

"Yeah, Mama. That's his fine ass. Hey, cousin-in-law,"

my cousin, Duchess, said. Duchess, formally known as Darryl, was my flamboyantly gay cousin. He was just like his damn mama. Loud as hell. I could always count on him to embarrass the hell out of me whenever we were out in public. His ass was beyond crazy, but I loved his crazy ass.

"Can you two please calm down? This is her event for her business." Thank God my cousin Keshyra was there. She was the calm one. She knew how to have a good time but she also knew how to be seen and not heard. Teeny Boo and Duchess knew nothing about that.

Sighing deeply, I said, "Karter, this is my auntie Tina and my cousins Keshyra and Darryl." Lord, why did I just give him their government names?

"Oh no, niece, you tried it." My aunt stood up from her seat, completely embarrassing me. This lady was wearing an all-white velour jump suit with a white boa wrapped around her arms. At least she stuck to the color scheme.

"Hey, baby, I'm Lauriel's fine ass auntie Teeny Boo." She reached in to hug my man, and him being the gentleman he was, he accepted. She held on to him a little too long.

"Damn, niece. He strong and fine."

"That's right, mama!" Duchess said, reaching up to give Teeny Boo a high-five. Then he looked towards me and gave me the death stare.

"My name ain't no damn Darryl. My name is Duchess. You better act like you know." He went over to stand by his momma and they started doing the bump.

Poor Keshyra looked embarrassed and my mother was just plain fed up.

"Teeny Boo, sit your ass down. That boy don't want you touching all over him. This is a professional event for my child. You better act like you got some sense." Then she looked at Duchess and said, "You too, boy. She knows what your damn name is, but you just met that child. Give him a minute before you show out. Damn."

Both of them sat down and shut up. My mother was the older sister and she loved her baby sister. She would do absolutely anything for her and her children, but my mama didn't tolerate acting an ass in public.

"Sorry, Teedy. You know my mama start me to acting up and I lose my mind," Duchess said to my mother. As loud and obnoxious as my cousin was, he had some great taste. He wore an all-white Versace shirt with the white pants and the white gators. He looked damn good, but I would never admit it and buck his head up even more. Although he was flamboyant, he still maintained his masculinity. Many women think he's a fine ass straight man until he opens his mouth. Keshyra looked just as beautiful with an off-white mermaid dress that flared out at the ankles. She was a pretty brown skin young woman.

"Well, mama, let me go to the stage and thank my guests for coming." Grabbing Karter's hand, I pulled him to come with me. I wasn't leaving him over here alone.

"It was nice meeting you all."

"Nice meeting you too, baby. I expect to see you at Sunday dinner this week." I knew that was a warning to have him with me this coming Sunday. And because it wasn't football season, there was no excuse for him not to be there.

"Yes, Ma'am. I'll be there."

Walking towards the stage, I heard Karter say, "Bae, your mama seemed like the only sane one in your family."

He burst into laughter.

"Aye, don't come for my Teeny Boo and my cousin. They might be crazy as fuck but neither of them play about me." He looked at me and put his hands up in surrender.

"Duly noted." Then he placed a kiss on my lips.

"Sis! You're here. Finally." I turned in the direction of my sister's voice.

Taniece looked so pretty. She was wearing a fitted baby tee with my company logo on the front along with some white jeans and some royal blue pumps. I knew she was going to throw some color in somewhere and it was ok because she worked damn hard to make this event happen.

"Yeah, we just got here about twenty minutes ago. I just introduced him to mama and them." She jerked her head in Karter's direction.

"Aww lawd, you met Teeny Boo?" Like he had proven a point from his previous statement, he started laughing again.

"Anyway. I'm going on the stage and thank everyone for coming. Did all the VIPs come?"

Looking over her clipboard, she said "Yes. They're all here and wearing Glamour Shoes."

"That's amazing. Ok, after I make this speech, I want you to come with me to go talk to them and thank everyone." She looked shocked that I said that. I wasn't sure why. Taniece was a part of the reason I am so successful. She helped me in every way possible. She was going to get as much of the praise as I was.

I walked up to the stage while Karter and Taniece stood to the side.

"Good evening, everyone, and thank you for coming to the launch party for the fall line of Glamour Shoes. I'm so happy for you all to see how hard my team and I have been working to give you all shoes designed especially for you. For the last five years, I've dedicated my life to my dream of designing shoes. I've always loved everything about creating something new for the world. I'd like to start by thanking the person that stands by me day in and day out, making sure everything moves effortlessly. My sister, Taniece. I appreciate you so much. Your drive pushes me to continue to be the big sister that you can be proud of, and I promise, if you stick with me, all your dreams will come true. I'd like to thank my mother for showing me what work ethic is. I learned so much from watching you work so hard for us and I love you so much for it. Last but certainly not least-" I heard the door to the ballroom slam and I was slightly thrown off from watching my best friend walk in wearing a bright red, skin tight, wrap dress. I briefly looked in my sister's direction and I noticed her pissed of expression she wore on her face.

Quickly composing myself, I said, "Last but not least, I'd like to thank my boyfriend, Karter. In the short time we've been together, you've been encouraging, caring, loving and everything else a great man can be. Thank you for being all that and more." I blew a kiss in his direction.

"Now, with that said, I want you all to see the shoes we have on display for you guys and enjoy the night. Thank you." Walking off the stage, I quickly bypassed my sister and my boyfriend to go confront my inconsiderate ass best friend.

Wasting no time and not evening bothering to give a warm greeting, I said, "Really, Jream?"

Jream

"Really, Jream?" Lauriel said to me with a pissed off look on her face.

"Really what?" Before she could answer, her pitbull answered for her.

"You know what, bitch. I know damn well when I sent you the invitation. It said guests are to where all white on the invite." Rolling my eyes upward, I saw what the invitation said, but I didn't think that included me.

"That's what you're mad about? Girl, it's not that big of a deal," I said dismissively.

"It is that big of a deal. I wanted everyone to wear white because I was supposed to stand out. This is my company. And obviously one of you got the memo because Noah followed instructions perfectly."

I looked in Noah's direction and got slightly pissed off. I told him to match the color I was wearing, but he kept saying he was following what the invite said. Not I. Nobody told me what to wear or when to wear it.

"Well, it's too late now. I'm here. I must have missed

the part where you thanked me."

"No, you didn't miss it. I didn't mention you." Before I had the chance to say anything smart back, I saw my baby approaching. He looked so fucking good in the color blue. My skin started to crawl when he reached out and wrapped his arms around that bitch Lauriel.

"Hey, Karter," I said in my sweetest voice.

Turning his attention from Lauriel, he said, "Hey, Jream. How are you?"

"I'm good. It's nice seeing you again. You look great." I know it's fucked up that I didn't bother extending a compliment to Lauriel, but who gave a fuck? This man was a walking orgasm.

"Karter, have you met Noah? He's Jream's boyfriend. Noah, meet Lauriel's man, Karter Montegue," Taniece said while staring at me. Noah extended his hand to Karter and he accepted the gesture.

That bitch knew what she was doing. I had absolutely no intention of introducing them. My soon to be ex-boyfriend did not need to meet my next boyfriend.

"Hey, man, nice meeting you. I'm a huge fan," Noah

said like a fucking groupie. I was embarrassed. I should have left his weak ass at home. I knew he wouldn't know how to act.

While he and Karter started to spark up a conversation, I heard Lauriel say, "Taniece, let's go speak to the VIPs. I really want to see how Inayah Lamis looks in her shoes."

My ears perked up at hearing a celebrity's name.

"I'll come with you guys too." Straightening my dress, I got ready to follow them.

"No, Jream, you stay here. This is a business conversation, not personal." Lauriel didn't even bother waiting for a comeback. She pulled Taniece along in the area where her VIPs sat.

The nerve of this bitch to tell me I didn't need to go with her. She must have obviously forgotten who the fuck I was. The position of baddest bitch in New Orleans was once held by me. Yea, I needed to get my shit together and get back on top. Clearly, it must have slipped her mind that things weren't always like this, but I was more than ready to remind her.

Looking at Noah made me disgusted. He had made me

fall from my pedestal. I was at the top of my socialite game when we were first together, now I couldn't even get an invite to a D list social event. It was time to put my plan in motion.

Walking up to Noah and Karter, I said, "Noah, do you mind getting me something to drink please?"

"Sure, babe. I'll be right back." Watching him walk away, I looked towards Karter. I figured now is the best time to set my plan in motion.

"Hi, Karter."

Pulling his eyes from the direction Lauriel was in, he looked at me and said, "Hey, wassup." I couldn't say enough how fine this man is. The things I planned to do to him are downright sinful.

"I figured this was as good a time as any to get to know my best friend's man. You know I'm the closest person to Lauriel." I wanted to gag on my own words, but this is what I had to do to get the job done.

"Oh really? I thought the closest person to her was her sister."

"Well, let's just say I know more of her secrets than

Taniece does," I said, looking him dead in his eyes.

"Is that right?" He looked intrigued.

"Absolutely. Look, I just want to tell you to be good to her. I don't want you to end up like the last guy." I looked away shyly.

"The last guy? What you mean?" I could tell by his line of questioning he wanted to know more but didn't want to ask.

"Aww shit, I've said too much. Nevermind. Don't worry about it. Look, you should take my number down." I quickly called my number out to him. "If you feel like you need a listening ear when it comes to Lauriel, I'm always here. Sometimes she can be a handful," I said while placing my hand on his bicep. Karter's muscles are so fucking strong. I can't wait until the day this man scoops me in his arms and fucks me against the wall.

"Yeah, I'll do that," he said with confusion. I knew I put a bug in his ear and I made him wonder what all Lauriel was keeping from him. If my plan worked like I was hoping it would, he would think about this shit all night and the moment he had an ounce of doubt, I'll be the first person he called.

Noah bought me my drink and looked at me skeptically.

"What was that about?"

"Nothing. I was just getting to know him a little bit."

"It looked like more than that to me."

"What are you insinuating?" I dared him to question me.

"You know what, Jream, fuck it. I'm getting real sick of your shit." With that said, he walked off.

I was shocked he reacted in such a way but ask me if I care. By the time we leave and get home, he'll be over it and my plan will still be in effect.

Noah Baptiste

Walking away from Jream was a first for me. Usually, it's her that's walking away from me. With each passing day, I was getting sick of her shit. I didn't know what the fuck her problem was, but she needed to get it together real quick.

All of this shit was becoming too much for me. From the moment I met Jream, I bent over backwards making sure she was happy and had everything she could ever ask for. She never had to lift a finger as long as I was around. That was the kind of man I was. I watched my father cater to my mother for the whole forty-five years of their marriage. The only difference between my mother and Jream, my mother catered to my father and appreciated him. When I had all that money, blowing it away on Jream, she was the happiest she could possibly be. It wasn't until the money dried up that I started to see her for who she really was.

The only reason I decided to open up my own business was because the moment my son came into this world, I wanted him to have something that was solely for him. Something I could pass down to him when the time came. Shit had been rough the last few years, but I was working my ass off to make shit better for us.

I had a plan that I was following and so far, I was right on schedule. But the plan didn't include my woman spending a fuck ass amount of money on bullshit like her hair. I wanted to break her fucking neck for that shit, but that wasn't my style. I'm starting to believe she sees me as a punk ass nigga and that's why she handles me like that. It's cool because I'm gonna start putting my foot down with her ass.

Throwing back my second shot of Hennessy, I felt someone tap me on my shoulder.

"Hey, Noah. What's up with the long face?"

I was graced with Taniece's beautiful face. I really hated to have these thoughts about my girl's friend, but this was one beautiful ass woman. I knew I was ten years her senior, but you couldn't tell that by how she carried herself. From the time I met both Lauriel and Taniece, I could tell they had their heads on straight. For the life of me, I couldn't understand why that shit never rubbed off on Jream. I loved her, I really did, but it seemed like she thought her only mission in life was to be taken care of. I tried not to complain because I had a lot to do with why she's like she is. Besides her parents, I contributed to her lazy behavior. That's one thing about our relationship I wish I could take back.

"Hey, T. I'm good, just enjoying the free liquor," I said with a laugh.

"I'll take your word for it. I just came over here to check on you."

"What do you when you're giving everything you've got but it's obviously not enough?" I said before I could catch myself.

She stopped in her tracks and looked at me softly.

"It depends. If you feel like it's worth it to keep giving, don't stop doing what you're doing. But only you can make the decision if you think you're giving too much and not receiving anything," she said to me truthfully.

I sighed heavily. "I don't know much about anything anymore, T. I'm doing the best I can."

She put her hand on my shoulder and said, "Sometimes it's not you that's the problem. I wish you could see what everyone else saw in you." With that, she walked away quickly.

Part of me wondered what she meant by that, but I didn't have the energy to run behind her and find out. A nigga was stressed out and it didn't help much that I was sitting in the corner, staring across the room, watching my woman making googly eyes at her best friend's nigga.

*

The drive home from Lauriel's launch party was a quiet one. After watching Jream prance around the room and slyly flirt with Karter all night, a nigga had too much shit on his mind. She was really subtle with her shit, but I knew her well enough to know what she was doing. I had never been an insecure nigga, and why should I be? I was a good ass man to my woman. Why would she stray? For the first time, I was seriously questioning our relationship.

"Why are you so quiet?" She asked as if she cared.

"Just got a lot on my mind." I decided to keep it short and sweet. I really didn't feel like arguing. I'd had a few drinks tonight and I just wanted to get home, shower and go to bed. Having a meaningless conversation with Jream wasn't on my list of things to do right now.

"Goodness, Noah. Can't we have one night where you aren't worried about your stupid business? We had a nice night tonight. Act like it." This motherfucker was going to make me strangle her.

"First of all, I'm not sitting here thinking about my business. And stupid? Despite the hardships I've been dealt over the years, my stupid business still takes care of your ungrateful ass."

"Barely!" She said with a huff.

"Jream, if I were you, I would kindly shut the fuck up because I'm getting really sick of your bullshit." She jerked her head in my direction like she couldn't believe my audacity. Well, in this moment, I didn't give a fuck what I said or how she felt. I felt like it was high time I got everything I needed to say off my chest.

"For the last five years, I have given your inconsiderate ass everything you wanted and needed. I haven't expected you to give me anything in return. The only thing I ever asked of you was to be patient with me, give me time to get my business off the ground and I would give you more than everything you could ever asked for. All you had to do was be a good mother to our son and you can barely do that. Meanwhile, I have to sit at a function for your best friend and watch you drool over her nigga. Ain't that a bitch!" She gasped heavily.

Did I hate that I said that to her? No. I bit my tongue about a lot. The fact that she was a part time mother ate at me worse than anything. Nyjae spent more time with my parents then he did with his own mother. If they didn't have him, he was with Lauriel or Taniece.

Jream did the minimal for our son. At first, I honestly thought it was postpartum depression that made her not want to interact with Nyjae. Instead of even questioning it, I took care of the things she didn't want to do. I did my best to be there for her for whatever I thought the problem may have been. Any time I asked her what the problem was, she would always tell me she was fine. Despite her mothering or lack thereof, that didn't stop her from spending all my damn money and the sad part is, I didn't stop her. I loved Jream and I was willing to do anything to make sure she knew I loved her. I just didn't realize, until recently, she was taking that shit for granted.

"Nigga, don't you dare question my mothering skills with your weak, broke ass! I wasn't drooling over anybody. But if I was, he got to be much better than your ass. Maybe I'll actually cum with another nigga. I'm sick of your pathetic, limp dick ass." Instead of saying anything more, I gripped the steering wheel tightly so I wouldn't say something that I would regret. That shit pissed me off more than I wanted to admit. Normally, I let a lot of shit roll off my back but I'll be damned if I let this shit ride tonight.

About two minutes later, we pulled up in the parking lot of the apartment complex. As soon as the car was in park, Jream jumped out the car and slammed my damn door. Her stupid ass must have forgotten I had the keys because she was standing there huffing and puffing with her arms folded. I didn't give a damn how mad she was, I was going to take my damn time walking to that door.

After I opened the door, she ran inside and ran straight to the bathroom. I didn't have the energy to deal with her bullshit right now, so I went to the kitchen and poured me another shot of henny. While I sat and thought more about the bullshit she said in the car, I got even more pissed off. That girl didn't appreciate a fucking thing I did for her. I never complained about how tired I was or even what I needed to be happy. I just wanted to make her happy. I swear, I couldn't win for losing. It was time I showed her ass it was time to stop fucking with me.

I walked in the bedroom and saw she was coming out of the bathroom. Since she had the nuts to call me limp dick, I was about to show her ass.

Standing there wearing one of my t-shirts and nothing else, she said, "What do you want, Noah? I don't have time for you sh-," Before she could finish, I grabbed her ass and pulled her close to me. Before she could let some fly shit come out of her mouth, I kissed her hard on the mouth. Rubbing my hands up and down her curves, I turned her ass around and started kissing and sucking on her neck while grabbing a handful of her breast.

"Noah, what are you doing?"

"Shut the fuck up and bend that ass over!" I said with

87

a hard slap to her ass.

Looking over her shoulder, she thought she was being sexy by the way she was taking that shirt off, but I was already disgusted with her ass. I was only doing this because I had a point to prove. Climbing on the bed, getting on all fours, I smacked her ass one more time before I loosened my pants to let them fall. Without so much as a warning, I plunged all seven inches deep inside her pussy. There was no point in being gentle. She thought I was a pussy, I was going to show just how much of a pussy I wasn't.

"Fuck, Noah! Just like that baby! Harder!" Fucking Jream with long deep strokes, I gripped her hips to make her fuck me back.

No matter how pissed I was, I couldn't deny how the shit felt, but I was determined to not be that limp dick ass nigga she said I was.

Listening to her groaning let me know she was enjoying it. In the midst of our fuck session, I closed my eyes and there she was. The girl that invaded my thoughts more than I wanted to. Her beautiful, blemish free, chocolate face. That fucking smile that made the whole room smile. Man, I had no business thinking about Taniece while I was fucking my woman, but that shit was happening more and more. I had no clue why she was playing like a movie in my head but I couldn't help it.

"Noah, baby! I'm about to cum! Right there, baby, don't stop."

In my head, I was hearing Taniece's voice, not Jream's and that shit was taking me over the edge.

"I'm cumming, baby! Fuck!" Hearing her scream and feeling myself about to nut, I quickly remembered where I was. I pulled out and came all over her ass. That was a first in our relationship. Normally, I would wear a condom because I didn't want to take the risk of making another baby. Jream didn't want to get on birth control because she was afraid the shot would make her fat. She didn't want an IUD nor did she think she would remember to take the pill. So, condoms was our only option. In the haste of trying to prove a point, I forgot to put one on.

"Why the fuck would you cum on my ass, nigga? That's some disrespectful shit. The fuck is wrong with you?" She looked at me disgusted.

Completely ignoring her, I said, "You're what's wrong with me! I come home every fucking day to a dirty ass house, my son needing to be bathed and fed. I never have a home cooked meal. But you want me to be able to fund your entire lifestyle and fuck you all night long. Motherfucker, please! That's some disrespectful shit."

"If you feel that way, then why the fuck are you here?"

Looking at her like she done lost her fucking mind, I couldn't help but think about what she said. The only excuse I could come up with was that I loved Jream, and I loved my son. Nyjae was my heart and I wanted to give him everything I had growing up. I got to witness my parents share and express their love every day of my life. I felt like Nyjae deserved the same.

"You know what, I don't even fucking know," with that said, I walked out of the bedroom and decided to sleep on the sofa tonight. I needed to think about a lot of shit and I didn't need to hear her huffing and puffing while doing so.

Karter Montegue

I had been thinking about what Jream had said for a few days now. That shit was bothering me to no end. I never bought it up to Lauriel because I didn't know how to. A part of me had been feeling like this shit was too good to be true. My baby and I vibe on a whole different level. We can talk about everything under the sun, she doesn't nag me about stupid shit, and I can already tell she's going to be my biggest fan as soon as football season starts. Lauriel made me want to give her a reason to love me.

Being a professional football player, the women we encounter only see one thing when they look at us. That's the type of hoes that you fuck and duck without thinking about it. Shit, I hadn't had a serious relationship since before I got in the league. These hoes in New Orleans be ready to throw themselves at you and for the most part, I catch what they're throwing. I was a firm believer in safe sex. As long as I strapped up faithfully, there would be no issue. I was always direct. I didn't make promises I had no intentions on keeping. I also didn't lie to kick it. Before I put my dick in anybody, they knew nothing more was coming from me but some dick.

The day I met Lauriel, I wasn't expecting to meet the woman I would want to spend my life with. She was just so fucking beautiful. Her body was amazing to me and she was so talented. When I had my assistant get me some custom shoes made, I was highly impressed by the outcome. After we formally met and got to know one another, I enjoyed her personality. I felt like the luckiest nigga when she agreed to be mine. Now, after almost four months of being together, I thought I knew everything about her.

That small conversation I had with Jream had my mind fucked up. I needed to know what she meant before I even thought about bringing that conversation to Lauriel.

Today, I had decided to call Jream and ask her out to lunch so she could elaborate on what she started to say the other night. Obviously, if Lauriel hadn't told me yet, then she just wasn't ready to. But it had to be important if her best friend let something slip.

I was on my way there, driving on the interstate when

my phone started ringing.

"Hello?"

"Hey, baby!" Lauriel said in her sweet voice.

"Wassup, Bae. You okay?"

"Yea, I was just calling while I had a free moment. Just wanted to see how your day was going."

I don't know if it was me or my fucked-up ass nerves, but I was slightly paranoid. Like she was checking up on me or something.

"My day is going good. I'm headed to a meeting right now so I'll just see you tonight, bae." I hated to feel like I was rushing her off the phone. A nigga didn't want to feel guilty about having this conversation with my girl's best friend without her knowledge.

"Oh, ok. I guess. See you later." I could tell by the way she just hung up the phone that she felt some kind of way. I would deal with it later and get us back on track.

Pulling up to Copeland's of New Orleans, I found a parking spot so I could get out and get this conversation over with.

Sitting in the booth I requested from the hostess, I

waited on Jream to come. My mind was filled with the possibilities of what she could possibly tell me.

After sitting there for another ten minutes, I finally saw her walking towards me. She looked like she was walking on a runway wearing an orange, two-piece skirt set and matching heels with her hair cascaded down her back. She looked like she was dressed to impress. I couldn't deny her beauty if I wanted to.

"Hi, Karter. How are you?" She reached in to give me a hug, which kind of threw me off. This girl didn't know me that well to be hugging me, but it wasn't that serious to be speaking on.

"Wassup, Jream. I'm good. How are you?"

"I'm amazing now that I'm here," she said, looking at me while tucking some of her hair behind her ear. I wasn't quite sure what that meant so I didn't bother asking her to elaborate.

"That's great." Taking a deep breath, I said, "Look, let me just cut to the chase. I asked you here because of what you said that night of the party. About how you didn't want me to end up like the last guy. What did you mean by that?"

"Oh, that." She rolled her eyes upward. Then said, "Can I keep it real with you?" She asked, looking me square in the eyes.

"Yeah, sure."

"Lauriel doesn't know how to be monogamous. As soon as she feels like you're getting too serious, it's going to be on to the next one. Which is why I said I didn't want you to end up like the last guy. The last man she was with, she hurt him so bad, he went crazy and almost killed himself." She looked away sadly then looked back at me. "I really don't want that for you."

What the fuck? This was the first I had ever heard about this shit. The most Lauriel had ever told me about an ex was about the dude that cheated on her. She ain't tell me shit about her ex nigga almost killing himself over her. The fuck?

"Jream, this the first time I done heard about this shit." I was looking at her skeptically. I couldn't believe the shit she was saying.

"Karter, I love my best friend, but is she really the woman for you? You need a woman that knows how to treat you, knows how to cater to you, and can conduct herself in your world. Lauriel isn't that girl. Plus, with her having her little business, can you really say she'll have time to be there for you like you need her to?"

Damn. I was shocked that my girl's best friend would say the things she was saying. Sadly, it made me think about what she said. I hated that she had me second guessing my baby, but I was. I loved Lauriel, but she was always busy. This was something I knew when we met. She didn't hide how important her business was to her. Right now, it didn't bother me because I had a lot of time on my hands because it was the off season. Minicamp and practice would start in a couple months, so I wondered how available she would be for me then.

"Damn, you just gave me an earful." A nigga was rendered speechless.

Coming over to sit next to me from the other side of the booth, she put her hand on my thigh.

"Karter, I understand this is a lot to take in but it's really ok. I know you really have feelings for her, but I think I know just what you need." Right as the words left her mouth, her hand fell right on the top of my dick.

Jumping damn near out my skin, I slapped her hand away.

"What the fuck are you doing?"

"Karter, it's ok. I'm exactly what you need, baby." She kept grabbing at my dick. I'm glad that I asked to be put in a private room when I got here. A lot of people liked to ask for autographs and although I didn't mind, I didn't like to be bothered while I was eating.

"Jream, get your hands off me. I don't want you girl. Stop. Fuck!" This bitch was strong as fuck. She had managed to pull my fucking zipper down, and I had no clue how she did it.

In one swift motion, she was on her knees and had my dick in her mouth.

"Ahhh, shit!" Don't get me wrong, I knew this shit was a mistake. This whole fucking lunch was a mistake. From the moment she opened her mouth to dog out my girl, I should have got my ass the fuck up out of here. She really had me questioning my entire relationship. Now, look at the position the bitch had me in, but I wasn't thinking with the right head right now. My dick was talking for me. Soon, it was going to be spitting down her throat.

Honestly, Jream didn't have shit on Lauriel. My baby head game was superb and this shit here was mediocre. But since she wanted my nut so bad, I was going to give it to her. Showing no mercy, I put my hand on the back of her head and fucked her face. She was enjoying this shit. Jream was moaning and groaning. It wasn't doing anything but making my dick harder. About five minutes later, I didn't even bother alerting her that I was about to spray my seed all in her mouth, I just let loose.

"Jream, get up girl." Finally getting my dick out of her mouth with a sound of a pop, she sat back up in her seat.

Wiping her mouth with the back of her hand, she looked at me curiously.

"See, baby. You can have that all the time. I'm exactly the woman you need, Karter."

Biting my lip, I tried not to laugh. Fuck, I couldn't help it. I burst out laughing directly in her face.

"Girl, I'm with the woman I need. This was a fuck up on my part. I asked you to come here thinking you were about to tell me some shit I really needed to know. All you did was shit on my girl and suck my dick. Now, you're trying to convince me that you're the woman for me. Don't you have a nigga?" I distinctly remember Taniece introducing me to a nigga that was supposed to be her boyfriend.

"You're with the woman you need? Nigga, you're weren't saying that when your dick was in my mouth," she said that shit like it made a difference to me.

"You damn right I wasn't. You wanted to suck my dick and I let you. Fuck out of here," I said with a wave of my hand.

"Oh really? Well, I wonder what Lauriel would say when I tell her you made me suck your dick," she said while looking down at her nails.

"She ain't gonna say shit because she's not gonna know." Finally getting out of my seat, I fixed my clothes to head out. It's time for me to get the fuck up out of here.

"If you don't give me what I want, she'll know."

"And what exactly do you want?" I don't know why I asked. Maybe just curious. But that's my fuck up because you know they say curiosity killed the cat.

"I want you, Karter. I deserve you! You deserve me." This girl was fucking hilarious.

"Let me make this shit real clear to you. You tell my woman what happened here today, and you gonna see a side that nobody's ever seen. Fuck with me if you want to."

Looking me directly in my face, she got up from the booth, fixed her clothes and hair, then said, "No, baby. You fuck with me if you want to. I'll be in touch."

As she moved to walk pass me, she blew a kiss in my direction.

Jream was one crazy bitch, I just didn't know how crazy.

Lauriel

Things had been crazy for the last couple of months. After my launch party, business had increased tremendously. Which meant Taniece and I were always busy, and my invoices stayed full. Getting recognition from All Tea, All Day, local celebrities and Instagram influencers, my business page was booming. We went from twenty thousand followers to almost two hundred thousand in a matter of weeks. Soon, I would need to hire a full staff to get my orders out in a timely fashion.

Everything seemed to be going well in my life. The only small snag I was experiencing was my relationship. Don't get me wrong, Karter and I were doing well, but he just seemed distant. I don't know what bought on the change, but I was a little worried. We were still spending great amounts of time together. I finally took him to Sunday dinner, and my entire family fell in love with him. Baby, when I tell you, he loved him some Mama and Teeny Boo. They can call him right now, and he will drop everything he's doing to go see what they need. They take damn good care of him too. Last week, that fool called my mama to cook him some greens and fried chicken. Now, I can cook. Hell, my mama taught me, but I think he loved just going over there and spending time with her since his mama is back in Cleveland. We were planning to go on a small vacation to go meet his family.

Even with all the beauty in our relationship, the distance I felt was bothering the hell out of me. Soon, he'd be going to minicamp and we'd both would be too busy to spend time together. I planned to spend the weekend catering to him and loving on him, but since today was Friday, I wanted to spend the night out with my girls. I even had extended the invitation to my cousins. They told me they would meet us there.

I had decided to end our day at the office early today so we could properly get ready for the night. It had been a while since I had been out with my sister and best friend. I hoped they could put the bull shit aside to have a great night tonight.

"I can't be fucked with, no. Ho you can't touch this, ay. Bitch, I do rich shit, huh. My money thick, thick, ay. Walk

with a limp, limp, huh. I'm on some pimp shit, ay. He say, You all about money, yeah. I'm on that cash shit, huh. I'm in my bag, bitch, huh. I'm on your ass, bitch, huh. I'm in that new, new shit. You on that last year, huh. Bitch, I do pimp shit, huh. Ho, you on simp shit, ay. He say, You all about money, yeah. I'm on that cash shit, ah. You know why these Bitches love me, cuz Baby don't give a fuck."

Fresh out of the shower, I had Alexa blasting *Cash Shit* by Megan the Stallion feat. Da Baby. It was the perfect song to put me in the mood to go out tonight. Even though I was in turn up mode, listening to Meg put me in business mode. It made me about what kind of shoe I can create that would signify her personal style.

Sitting in front of my vanity, I was getting ready to apply my makeup. Deciding to just go with a natural beat, I took my time moisturizing my skin. I used to be so apprehensive about my skin complexion years ago, now I love the skin I'm in. It took courage to rock this melanin and I rocked it with my head held high.

As soon as I was done with my makeup, I took my bonnet off my head and allowed my long, silk tresses to fall down my back. My hair was one trait I believed Taniece and I got from our father. If I was wearing weave, it was only because I felt like it. I didn't need it at all.

Slipping into my silver "Got a Thing for You" Cowl Neck Cami and shorts from Fashion Nova, I admired myself in my full-length mirror. This outfit was so simple yet classy and comfortable. I paired my outfit with some silver heels that were spiked on the heel of the shoe but the straps were clear. Impressed with what I saw staring back at me, I was ready to enjoy myself for the night.

Walking out of the bathroom, I ran smack dab into Karter.

"Damn. Where are you going looking like that?"

I was slightly surprised to see him here. He hadn't called me to let me know that he was on his way over or anything like that. However, he did have a key to my place. A while back, I needed him to accept a package for me when he wasn't busy. I gave him a key for that reason, and I just never asked for it back. It didn't bother me that I didn't have one to his place yet. We spent more time at mine. And to be honest, I was more comfortable at my house.

I reached up to give him a hug and to place a kiss on his lips.

"Hey, baby. I'm about to head out to have a girl's night out with T and Jream. You forgot I told you about it?"

He sighed and said, "Yeah, baby, I did. I had a long day today." I wrapped my arms around my man and I felt him tense up slightly.

"What's wrong, baby?" I was worried about him.

"I just had to meet with the front office today. The GM and my agents are in the process of negotiating my contract. My agent wants them to give me what he thinks I'm worth and shit, I do too. I just don't want to leave New Orleans. I ain't with playing for these other teams." He had explained to me before that he loved the dynamic of his team. It took them some time to build the team they have now and that wasn't something Karter was ready to walk away from.

"I'm sorry, Karter. I know that has to be a lot on your shoulders." I began to rub his back to try and ease his stress.

"I mean, it's a part of the game. A nigga can get traded at any time. I just been here so long, my life is here. I enjoy playing here." Then he looked at me and said, "Baby, you're here."

We stared in each other's eyes like we were having a staring contest.

"Lauriel, hypothetically, what would happen to us if I got picked up by another team?" He looked deeply in my eyes waiting on an answer.

"To be truthful, baby, I never really thought about that." And the truth was, I hadn't. It may have been naïve of me, but it had never crossed my mind that Karter could possibly leave New Orleans. We were living in our own little world during this off season. Besides working out and a few work functions, we didn't have much to do with football. Now the real world was beginning. The possibilities were endless.

"Baby, I'm going to need you to think about this. You have to understand, my agent can call me tomorrow and tell me they didn't accept what we're asking but New England did. I'd be on a plane the same day. What would happen to us? Lauriel, a nigga love you and not trying to lose you." Karter grabbed my hands and held them tightly.

I honestly wasn't ready to even have this conversation. We'd been dating almost six months. Yes, we were getting serious, but I didn't know if we were that serious for me to follow him wherever he may be traded to. So, instead of answering him, I decided to try and change the subject.

"Baby, you seem really stressed. I know this is a conversation we need to have, but you need to relax. We can talk about all this after you've talked to your agent and find out where things seem to be going. Let's not worry about anything if we don't have to," I said, trying to deflect the conversation from that serious ass shit he wanted to talk about. I really needed time to think and I couldn't do that with him staring at me.

"You're right, bae. Go ahead and go out with your girls. Be safe and enjoy yourself." He kissed me softly on my forehead. "You look beautiful by the way," he said with a look of lust in his eyes.

"Thank you, handsome." Gathering my clutch and keys, I asked, "Are you going to be here when I get home?"

"Yeah, I'm about to shower and lay down. Call me when you're on your way. I need to know you're safe." He kissed me once more before I made my way outside.

Hopping in my car, I jumped on the interstate to go pick up my sister. Taking the twenty-minute ride to her apartment, I decided to ride in silence. Thinking about what Karter said plagued my mind. The fact that he could be traded actually scared me. What would happen to us? If I did follow him to another city and state, what would happen to my business? I didn't have the team just yet to run my business in another state. I was getting established, but damn, I wasn't there just yet. I always dreamed of the day I would be able to open another "Glamour Shoes" in a different state, but I couldn't do that anytime soon.

Finally pulling up to my sister's apartment, I texted her to let her know I was outside. About five minutes later, she came waltzing outside looking like a chocolate goddess. Sometimes, it amazed me how much my sister looked like me. She came outside wearing a pretty yellow halter dress and paired it with some gorgeous blue wedges. The colors looked so good up against her skin. She had her hair in its natural state. The curls framed her face to perfection.

As she jumped in the car, she said, "Hey, sis." Reaching over ,she kissed me cheek to cheek.

"Hey, baby girl. You look beautiful." Taniece was my heart. Even though we were five years apart, we were extremely close.

"You look bomb too, sis." She put her seat belt on and relaxed against my leather seats.

"I'm so happy you decided to get out tonight and have a good time. It's been a while since we've done this."

"Girl, tell me about it." She was right. I was always so focused on work, the only thing I really made free time for was Karter.

"You didn't tell me where we were going. You just told me to get ready."

"We're going to Masquerade." Referring to the club that was inside the Harrah's Casino of New Orleans. I just wanted to go someplace I knew I was guaranteed to have a good time.

Doing a little dance in her seat, I knew she would be excited to go. She liked to go gamble on the video machine because as long as you were gambling, you could drink for free.

"Text Duchess and Keshyra and let them know we are on our way."

As if I almost forgot, I snapped my fingers and made one more request.

"Text Jream too and let her know that we're on our way so she can meet us there."

Watching my sister stare at me from the corner of my eye, I let out a deep sigh.

"Taniece, please don't start. We all deserve a night out. I just want to enjoy it with my sister and my best friend."

I heard her mumble under her breath. "That bitch ain't your friend." But she still pulled her phone out and did what I asked her to do.

"She said she's on her way." T put her phone up then folded her arms.

"Girl, fix you face. We are going out to have a good time. Stop being jealous. You know you're my favorite person."

"Bitch, I am not jealous. I'm your sister. That hoe can't

take my place. It just pisses me off that you don't see this girl for who she really is." For as long as I could remember, Taniece had been telling me that Jream wasn't my real friend. I knew that the girl was self-centered as fuck, but she had been my girl for over a decade. Jream and I had a friendship that others wouldn't understand. And although things had changed as the years rolled by, she was still my girl.

"Taniece, I've told you this time and time again, Jream is my friend and will remain my friend until she gives me a true reason why she shouldn't be." I knew some of the shit Jream did was questionable to my sister, but a lot of shit didn't bother me. So far, there was nothing too bad that could stop me from being her friend.

"What about her blatantly coming to your launch party in that loud ass color when you know she knew what color she was supposed to wear."

I took a minute to actually think about what she said. When Jream showed up to my party with that loud ass red dress on, it did more than pissed me off; it hurt me. I've always known that Jream was an inconsiderate person, but not with me. This was me we were talking about. Lauriel. Her best friend that had been ten toes down from the beginning. Why would she show out at some shit that was for me? I also watched how she was interacting with my man. She never made me feel like I had to step to her about it though.

"Look, Taniece. Good friends are hard to come by. You know me. I don't do new bitches. At all. I'm not stupid, sis. I knew the bullshit Jream pulled the other night and her being ignored and not the center of attention, hurt her worse than I ever could." I touched my sister's arm so she could know I was serious. "If the day ever comes that she shows me anything other than her being genuine, I'm gonna kick that bitch to the curb."

Instead of commenting on my statement, she just looked out the window and we continued on our way to the casino.

After parking in the parking garage, we made our way inside, ready to enjoy the night. It was a little after eleven pm so the night was still young. While we waited on Jream, we decided to play on some of the machines before going in the club. We played on the video black jack table and enjoyed the free drinks until our cousins and Jream finally showed their asses up.

"Cousinnnnnn!" I heard Duchess' loud mouthed ass from a mile away. He and Key were making their way towards us looking fabulous as fuck. Duchess' favorite brand was Versace so he was rocking a black and gold Versace shirt with the black pants and black loafers. Keyshara was simply dressed in a white halter top and some high waisted, stone washed, ripped jeans. She matched her outfit with some white pumps. She looked so cute.

"Loud mouth ass hoe," Taniece said next to me. I fell out laughing because she was worse than my mama. She hated when they got loud and common in public.

"I heard that lil bitch! Don't let the bougie fool you." He did a spin move to shut shit down. He was an absolute mess.

"Hey, ya'll!" Key said sweetly. I loved my baby cousin because she was so sweet and humble. Keshyra was in her second year of college and doing amazing. I always told her when she was ready to get to work, come see me. At the moment, she just wanted to focus on her studies.

"Ya'll ready to go inside? I'm ready to shake my ass. I've been working hard at the salon all week, I needed this night out." Duchess had a booth at a salon in uptown New Orleans. He was good at what he did and he stayed booked and busy.

"We're about to go inside. We're just waiting on Jream."

"No, you're waiting on Jream," Taniece said.

"Uhhh. That hoe coming?" Duchess said with an attitude.

"Yes, do you have a problem with that?"

"Nope. If you don't mind her fake ass coming out to party with us, then I don't mind either." I knew his ass was being shady. Duchess was another one that didn't too much care for Jream. He always said it was something about her he didn't trust and I always told him the same thing I told Taniece. She was my friend. End of story.

Before I could say anything to him, I saw her come around the corner. She looked really pretty but a little on the hoochie side. She was wearing a soft pink short set, cat suit. The outfit had long sleeves and a plunging neckline. She matched her outfit with some black thigh high boots. It wasn't my forte whatsoever, but I didn't knock her.

"Hey, girl, you look pretty," I told her as soon as she came towards us.

She flipped her hair over her shoulder and said, "I know."

I was completely taken aback by what she said. This girl came out with a funky ass attitude.

"Damn, bitch, you don't know how to take a compliment." She looked away and rolled her eyes.

Duchess looked like he wanted to say something, but Key grabbed his arm to stop him. He may not have listened to many people when they wanted him to quiet down, but he did listen to his baby sister.

"Girl, fuck you and your attitude. Come on, sis. Let's go in the club and have some fun," said Taniece. Too bad I didn't have the same effect on my sister. She had a few of those drinks and now she was feeling it. Not waiting for Jream to say anything more, T pulled my hand so we could go in Masquerade.

"Fuck him, then I get some money. Fuck him, then I get some money. I need tongue, I need face. Gimme brain, concentrate. Apple phone, Prada case. Kill a weave, rock a lace."

As soon as we walked in, we heard *No Limit* by G Eazy feat. Cardi B and Asap Rocky.

We started dancing and enjoying the music while Jream stood by the stage looking pissed off. I didn't have time for her bullshit. She should have stayed her ass at home. I was going to enjoy myself then go home and fuck my man until I pass out.

After a few more songs and we were still on the floor, they started playing the bounce version of SWV's *You're the One*. It seemed like at that moment, Jream finally came over to us and started dancing. I don't know what my girl was feeling, but she was singing her heart out.

"I know that you're somebody else's guy, but these feelings that I have for you I can't deny. She doesn't treat you, the way you want her to. So come on stop running, I want to get with you. What your girl don't know won't hurt

*her. Anything to make this love go further. You're the One,
You're the One for me.* "

She started dancing around me, then she bent over and
started shaking her ass. I thought it was hilarious. I was
enjoying myself so much and was glad I finally made the
time to come out with my cousins, sister and best friend.

After another hour of dancing and enjoying the music,
we decided to finally go get something to eat. Hopping in
our separate vehicles, we hopped on the interstate to go to
our favorite late-night spot in the 7th ward, Melba's. This
place had the best soul food. Any time I went, I would
always get the cabbage, baked chicken and corn bread.
Keshyra called me and told me they were going to head
home because Duchess had to work in the morning. I told
her how glad I was they came out with us and we had to
make it happen again soon.

After driving for less than ten minutes, we pulled up in
the packed parking lot, got out and went to stand in line to
order our food. We all placed our orders and sat down in
the dining area to wait for our orders to be called. My poor
sister was buzzing for real so she was sitting at the table

with us, chilling with a goofy grin on her face.

"I had so much fun tonight, I'm glad we decided to get out of the house. These last few weeks have been stressful." I sighed in slight frustration. I didn't want to complain because things could really be worse, but everything that had been bothering me was on my mind at the present moment.

"What's been going on best?" Jream asked in curiosity. I'm not gonna lie, it had been a while since she and I had sat down and talked about what was going on with either of us. I had been so busy with work and Karter that I didn't have much time for anything else. I'd barely checked on my godchild. I was feeling like a bad friend.

"Girl, just small things. Taniece and I have been putting in a lot of extra hours at Glamour. So, we're kind of exhausted. And, things with Karter kind of took a turn." At the mention of hearing Karter's name, it seemed like Jream's eyes lit up. As quick as the look happened, it faded just as quickly.

"What do you mean? Trouble in paradise?"

"No, I wouldn't say that. He's just been dealing with a

lot with his agents and his team's front office. Just feels like we've been distant lately."

Jream looked at me with a weird expression before saying, "Maybe he's realizing with the season starting soon, he doesn't really need to be tied down in a relationship."

As soon as the thought crossed my mind, I quickly ignored it. "I don't think that's it."

"Why not? Think about it. You guys met in the off season. He's going to be going back out on the road soon. There's tons of beautiful woman out there. Why would he just settle for a relationship with you?" Well damn. That was some fucked up ass shit to say.

"Damn, Jream. Bitch, shouldn't you be giving me advice on how to help my relationship? Not tell me that my nigga might not want to be with me so he can have his pick of the groupie bitches." She had just pissed me off with that bullshit. I couldn't understand this bitch for the life of me. I would never handle her like that. Whenever she was complaining about Noah, I encouraged this motherfucker. She wanted to berate a damn good man, and I would always try to encourage her to fight for him. I just couldn't understand why she couldn't give me the same.

"Why would you say something like that?" I asked Jream.

Before she could respond, Taniece said, "Because that bitch a hater."

Jream jerked her head in T's direction and said, "Excuse me?"

Taniece looked her square in the eyes and said, "Bitch, you heard me. You a fucking hater. What kind of best friend, a real fucking friend, would tell her home girl some shit like that? Bitch, with friends like you, who needs enemies."

"I ain't no fucking hater. I'm just being honest. The nigga about to be going out on the road soon. He's going to have access to millions of beautiful women, why settle for Lauriel." When that statement left her mouth, that was my last straw. I was tired of Jream's bullshit. Yeah, I considered her a friend, but this bitch was treading on thin ice.

"Bitch, he settling with me? Girl, fuck what you think.

That nigga met the best when he met me. That's more than I can say for poor Noah." She wanted to take shots, well I could take shots too.

"I know that's right," Taniece said in agreeance.

"Oh yea? That's how you feel?" She asked me as she took out her cell phone and started texting away.

"Well obviously that's how you feel. I've never kicked your ass while you've been down but the first time, in a long time, I choose to tell you what's going on with me, you say this shit. You know what..." I started getting up to leave out the store. I've lost my fucking appetite.

I gave Jream one last look. "When you find my best friend, tell her to find me. I don't know who this whack bitch is in my face. Taniece, let's go." Thankfully, my sister got up without giving me one of her smart-ass comments.

Getting back in the car and taking the drive to go drop my sister off, I was glad she didn't say much. I wanted to sit with my own thoughts and just get home to be held by my man.

I quickly dropped my sister off with an "I love you"

and a promise to call the next morning. Looking at the clock on my dashboard, I noticed it was almost three am, so I decided to call my man to let him know I was on my way home to him.

"Hello?" He answered sounding like he was moving around.

"Hey, baby. I thought you would have been sleeping."

"Yeah, I was. One of my homeboys called me. He got into some shit with his girl and needs me to come pick him up."

"At three in the morning?" I asked incredously.

He sighed in frustration. "I know, bae. Don't worry. I'll be back home soon."

"Ok, Karter. Be careful." With that, I hung up.

I was really aggravated now. I thought I was going to have a drama free night with my girls. It was anything but. All I wanted to do was go home, shower and lay in my man's arms. I couldn't even do that. My night had gone from sugar to shit, just that fast.

Jream

While sitting there fussing with Lauriel about our man's intentions for her or lack thereof, I pulled out my phone and sent that ole good text message.

Jream: Reserve a room at the Courtyard Marriot now.

I patiently waited on a text back, knowing they were going to be pissed at my request.

Karter: What? Fuck no!

Laughing at the text message, I slyly maneuvered my phone to take the picture I needed.

Jream: Think it's time I start telling our little secrets.

After pressing send, I knew that would get the response I was hoping for.

Karter: Meet me there in thirty minutes.

By now, Lauriel and her little minion have left me sitting here alone because she didn't like our conversation. Shit, it was true. Why would Karter want to settle for someone like her when he could have any beautiful woman in this world? Especially me.

Getting in my car to make my way to the hotel, I heard

my phone ringing. I rolled my eyes seeing that it's Noah.

"Are you on your way home?" He asked as soon as I answered.

"Actually no. I'm not coming home tonight."

"The fuck you mean you're not coming home tonight?" He sounded really pissed.

"Exactly what the fuck I said, I'm not coming home tonight. Taniece has been going through it with her lil boo, so I'm just going to keep her company tonight." The lie rolled off my tongue effortlessly.

"You're going to do what? You and T don't even get along that well," he said exactly what I know to be true.

"So what? She needs a friend and I'm going to be there for her." It was nauseating saying this stupid shit, but I needed an alibi for the night. One thing I knew, Noah wouldn't go calling anybody because, unfortunately for him, he trusted me.

"Jream, you have a man at home that's been waiting on you and wants to lay under you. Don't you think that's more important?"

I honestly didn't and I was going to tell him exactly

that. After the night of the party, the way Noah fucked my brains out, things had started getting a little better between us. I still wasn't getting the dick I wanted, but his would do for now. Soon, I got tired of faking the feelings I had for him, and shit went back to how it used to be. I simply didn't want his ass, but I would use him up until I was done with him.

"Honestly, no! My friend needs me and that's all there is to it." With that, I hung up in his face and blocked his number. I don't know why he even thought I was going to entertain his soft ass. It's not like my son needed me. I had dropped him off with his Noah's parents for the weekend so I was free to do what I wanted, and that didn't include having anything to do with Noah's ass.

After driving another ten minutes, I finally made it to the hotel and texted the person I was there to meet, asking for the room number. They sent the text about a minute later.

Getting out, I walked inside and bypassed the front desk, making my way to the room. Knocking on the door, I waited for a response. A couple of seconds later, the door opened and they let me in.

"What the fuck are you wearing?" He said in his deep voice. He started laughing before he could finish his question.

I looked down at my outfit, wondering what the problem was. I looked good in my catsuit.

"Whatever, nigga. It doesn't matter what I'm wearing. I bet your ass is here to see me," I said, waiting on a smart response.

"You didn't give me much of choice, now did you? Sending me that picture and shit," Karter said, looking me square in the eyes.

After the first encounter we had at lunch, we'd seen each other a few more times. Each time it was with me threatening to tell his bitch about me sucking his dick. So far, that's all he's allowed me to do, but I planned to change that tonight.

"Look, Jream, I know my ass ain't innocent here. You really need to stop this bullshit you doing. I love Lauriel." I rolled my eyes when he made that bullshit statement.

"You can't love her too much, you've been sneaking

off to see me." Karter knew what was up. He knew I wanted his ass and feeds right into my bullshit.

"You don't give me much of a choice, now do you? Any way. Why am I here?"

"Look, Karter, it's time to cut the bullshit. Despite the shit you say and how you act, you know you want me as much as I want you. Why continue playing with me?" As I was talking, I started removing my clothes. He didn't say anything as I slid my catsuit down my body. I was getting wet just from him watching me.

"Man, come on, Jream, Chill out with this bullshit." I knew his protest were bullshit because he never moved. I started walking closer to him

"No, you come on, Karter." I stopped in front of him, staring in his eyes while undoing his jeans.

His breathing started getting heavier as I pushed him back to sit on the bed. I kneeled down so I could take him in my mouth. I swear this nigga tasted so good. I don't know if it was the deceit of what I was doing that made me so fucking horny, or the thought of all the money he was going to spend on me.

I know, I know. The way I'm going about getting him is coming off a little ho-ish, but I don't fucking care. As long as I have the man at the end of the day, I'll do anything.

Karter had laid all the way back, enjoying the amazing head I was giving him. I had already devised my plan to kick this shit up a notch and I was ready to make it happen. I stopped sucking his dick long enough to reach inside of my purse to retrieve the condom I had. I tore the wrapper and slid it down his thickness. Before he could protest, I climbed on the bed, and slid him inside my wetness.

"Whoa, wait a minute." He tried to push me off him, but I was too strong.

"No, baby. Your dick feels too good for me to stop." I moved his hands from my hips to my breasts. I assume he started getting into it because he started kneading my nipples between his thumb and index finger.

"Shit!" Karter said quietly.

I moved to plant my feet on either side of him on the bed. Getting in the froggy style position, I started bouncing up in down, making sure his dick went in as deep as it could.

Smack! "Yes, baby! Do that shit." He smacked my ass again.

"Bounce that ass faster." I started bouncing up and down faster and coming down harder. I was on the verge of cumming.

"Oh shit, Karter, I'm so close to cumming! It's right there, daddy." I started grinding my hips so that the friction of our movement could get to my clit. That's all it took.

"Shit, shit, shit! I'm cumming!" He didn't have to tell me. He was coming too. I knew by the way he was pulling me down on his dick.

After it was over, we both were spent. I climbed off him to go clean myself up and to get a hot towel clean him off. I walked back out into the room. He was laid out on the bed with his eyes closed. I took the condom off then cleaned him off.

I don't think he realized how tired he was because he turned over and started snoring. I decided to lay down next to him and enjoy the moment for however long it was going to last. I heard a phone vibrating and it was his on the night stand. I reached over and saw my best friend calling his phone. I smirked at the irony that she was so confident that she had her man on lock, but he was sleeping next to me.

I snuggled closer to Karter, loved the feeling of being close to his body. I knew my dreams would be amazing thinking about the new little baby I hoped to be blessed with as a result of the condom I poked holes in.

Taniece

I couldn't believe that bitch had come for my sister the way she did. To basically tell Lauriel her relationship was rocky was because her man may feel like he settling for her, that was bullshit and that bitch knew it. I honestly didn't know what was going on. but I knew Karter loved my sister. The way his eyes lit up when she entered the room was noticeable. He didn't just tell her how he felt, he showed her. Even after a short time, their love was admirable. I hope God sent me a man that looked at me that way.

I was glad to be home after our night out. Before the bullshit, we hadn't had fun like that in a while and it made my night. Them drinks had me feeling nice and a shower would make me feel even better.

"Alexa, play *Am I Dreaming* by Ol Skool feat Xscape." Gathering my things to get in the shower, I began to come out of my dress and pin my hair up.

"Am I dreaming, am I just imagining you're here in my life? Am I dreaming? Pinch me to see if it's real cause my

mind can't decide."

I was enjoying the music as the hot water cascaded down my body. It felt so good and I just knew the sleep that was coming after was going to be even better. The only downfall of my night was that I didn't get my damn food. I was tweaking for that food man. That hoe Jream pissed my sister off so bad, I didn't even get a chance to eat.

The song had come to an end, but I wanted to end my night with music putting me to sleep. Getting out the shower, I wrap my fluffy white towel around my body.

"Alexa, play 90s R&B." I decided to go to my kitchen to make a sandwich.

Knock Knock

"Who the fuck beating on my door this time of night?" Going to the hall closet, I got my taser. My mama made sure Lauriel and I knew how to protect ourselves at an early age. She didn't play that shit. We were two beautiful, black, young women, living on our own. We needed to be able to handle our own.

Slowly walking to the door, I finally made it and asked, "Who is it?"

"It's Noah." What the fuck was he doing at my door at nearly four o'clock in the morning?

Opening the door, I looked at him skeptically.

"Hey, Noah. What's going on?"

Noah, my handsome friend... Noah looked stressed as fuck. It was just written all over his face. He had me worried about what could be wrong with him. He and I were still good friends, but it wasn't like him at all to just show up at my door unannounced, let alone this time of night. I could also tell that he'd been drinking. I could faintly smell it coming off him. Stepping aside, I let him in so I could find out what was going on.

"I know it's late and I'm sorry. Can you tell Jream I need to speak to her?" What the hell was he talking about? I know the look on my face had to be one of confusion because that's exactly what I was. Confused as all hell.

"Can't you call her yourself?"

"I would have, but I think she got me blocked. Every time I call, it goes straight to voicemail. Can you just go wake her up please?" He paused for a second then said, "I know this is some bullshit I'm bringing to your door, but I

133

didn't know what else to do."

"Well, I wish I could help but Jream isn't here." I went to go sit on my couch because I was already tired and standing up in the middle of my living room talking about Jream wasn't it right now.

"You can stop playing, Taniece. I know she told you to tell me that." In all honesty, it wasn't me to be ratting people out, but I didn't have an alibi to help Jream out. I honestly didn't want to but like I said before, I wouldn't purposely throw salt on her name.

"I'm really not playing, I'm here all by myself. Didn't you see that her car wasn't outside?" I honestly didn't have a clue as to why she would say she would be here.

"To be honest, I ran my ass to your door so fast, I didn't even look to see if it was outside. She just told me she would be here."

"Did she say why she was coming here? Maybe she just hadn't made it home yet." Noah looked exhausted as fuck. I guess he got tired of standing, so he fell next to me on the sofa with a small thud.

"Taniece, I don't know what the fuck is going on. This

girl got me so fucking stressed out and I have no clue what to do. I don't know how to make this shit better or even if I want to."

I sighed heavily because I honestly didn't feel like dealing with this. I didn't want to talk about Jream and her bullshit. This shit between her and Noah had been going on for a while and the truth was, the bitch didn't deserve him. The only time she was a good woman to him was when he had all the money in the world, but when that slowed up, the way she treated him did too.

"Look, Noah. I wish I had the answers to give you. If I did, I would help you. Shit, look at me, single as the day I was born. I don't know shit about relationships," I said with a laugh.

"Single? I thought you had a lil boo." Noah asked me while staring at me intently.

"A boo? Baby, who lied to you? I wish I did have a boo. It just hasn't happened yet. Someday though. No worries." I could feel Noah staring at me. His gaze was piercing through me, and it was making me nervous.

"Boy, why you looking at me like?" I asked nervously.

"Man, T, you just don't know how beautiful you are." I turned my head away from him because I felt myself blushing and I didn't want him to see that.

"Nah, man, I'm serious. You're not only beautiful on the outside, my nigga, you got a heart of gold. When the nigga that's for you comes around, he better cherish the ground you walk on, or he's gonna have to deal with me."

I looked towards Noah to see the seriousness written all across his face. He just didn't know, I wished he was the man he was referring to. I swear, I hated how I felt about this man, but I couldn't help it. He was everything a woman could ask for, but due to the circumstances, he just wasn't meant for me.

"I'm gonna go ahead and go back home. Maybe she's there." Walking towards the door, he turned around and said, "Thank you for letting me get some shit off my chest. I appreciate you for that." He reached in to give me a hug and I swear it was the best hug I've ever experienced in my life. The way he wrapped his arms around my body and held me tightly made me feel so safe and secure. The natural smell of his body made me dizzy with arousal. I needed to get him away from me before I couldn't control myself.

When he began to pull away, he looked down into my eyes. It felt like he was staring into my soul. I couldn't look away if I wanted to. He moved his head down towards mine, and let his lips graze mine. Another second later, I felt Noah press his lips firmly against mine. I knew I should have stopped it, but it was no use. The electricity coursing through our kiss was intense. Like a magnetic pull I had no control over. His tongue found its way inside my mouth and started doing its own special dance. The way Noah was kissing me should have been a sin. That's just how good it was.

After kissing for so long, Noah started giving me small pecks on my lips then moved down to my neck. From my neck, he started placing kisses down to my chest. He didn't waste any time pulling at my towel to make it fall to the floor.

"Damn," He said under his breath as I watched him admire my body.

Everyone liked to say that my sister and I looked just

alike, which was true, but I had the breasts she wanted. I loved my full thirty-eight C cup and I can see Noah does too. Before going any further, Noah quickly picked me up as if I were as light as a feather. I guess being five-four had its advantages. I wrapped my legs around him and allowed him to guide me down the hall to my bedroom, sharing another intense kiss along the way. When we made it to my room, Noah gently placed me on the bed and wasted no time opening legs and falling to his knees. I was nervous as hell but anxious to find out what his mind was telling him to do.

As if he didn't want me to think about it too long, he dove in head first in my kitty and began to eat her like she was his last meal. I had never in my life ever experienced anything like this before. I was mad at myself that I had waited this long. This shit was so fucking amazing, but no matter how good it felt, I knew what we were doing was wrong. I reached down to gently push Noah away by his shoulder.

"Noah, stop. We can't do this."

"Uh, uh," he mumbled while his head was still buried

in my wetness. "Don't make me stop, Taniece. You taste too fucking good."

"Shit!" My legs started trembling and it felt like my stomach was about to start cramping.

Noah raised my legs up by the back of my thighs and glided his tongue from my clit down to my ass crack. I was in so much shock from him doing such a thing, I looked down at him. He was staring at me like he needed me to know it was him giving my body the pleasure it was receiving. That did it for me. I placed my hands on the back of his head and pushed him deeper into my kitty. Grinding in his face, I needed this orgasm that was coming.

"Noah. Baby, I'm cumming! Damn, it feels so good." I went into mild convulsions before I fully calmed down.

When it was finally over and my body had calmed down, Noah was still sucking on my clit. It was so sensitive. He gave it one final kiss before he stood up. My whole fucking body was tired but that didn't stop me from watching him remove every article of clothing. When he dropped his pants, his dick seemed like it was a pretty decent size but the question was, was I ready? Did I want to share that part of me with Noah?

Before I could allow the words to fall out my mouth, he pushed my legs back open, put his body on top of mine and kissed me again. If I wasn't already feeling this man, his kisses alone would make me fall in love. Without hesitation, Noah tried to push his dick inside of me, but do to the fact that I was a virgin, he was met with a lot of resistance.

"Just relax, T, I got you baby. I promise."

Listening to him reassure me made it easier for me to allow him access. The first few strokes were painful as all hell, but the moment when he pushed all the way inside me, I bit my lip to try to keep from screaming. This was a bittersweet feeling. I was no longer a virgin. The pain felt unbearable but after a few more strokes, the pleasure became amazing.

"Damn baby, you so fucking tight. How long has it been?" He said in the middle his long, slow strokes. I knew he was asking me how long it had been since I had sex.

Deciding to be completely honest, I said, "Never."

Slowing his pace just a bit, he said, "Huh?"

Sighing heavily, I said, "I never had sex before." Seeing the shock on his face made me feel bad that I hadn't stopped him to begin with. Noah was the type of man that cared about the people in his life. I knew he would never hurt me on purpose and his reaction only showed me that more.

"What?? Nah, T. We can't-," I stopped him in the middle of his sentence with a kiss. He couldn't stop, I didn't want him to stop. I knew we were dead ass wrong, but it was too late to take it back at the moment. I'm a grown ass woman. I'll deal with the consequences later.

"Don't stop. Please don't stop. I know this isn't the ideal situation, but I don't regret you being the person I'm giving myself to." With that, I wrapped my legs around him and pulled him deeper inside me.

"Fuck..." He groaned as he continued his strokes. Looking me in my eyes, I assume looking for more assurance, I reached up to kiss him again. Our kiss intensified and didn't end.

Noah grabbed my hands and placed them above my head. His strokes became shorter and faster. He was making love to my mouth and my body at the same time and it was driving me absolutely insane.

"This pussy so fucking good. Shit so tight." Releasing my hands, he took his arms and wrapped them around me, holding me even closer to him.

"Come on, T. I feel that pussy tightening on my dick. Come for daddy, baby." I didn't know what was happening, but the pressure that was building up was entirely too much for me to handle.

"Move, Noah, I have to pee," I said to him but he wouldn't let me go.

"Nah baby, that ain't it. Gimme what I'm looking for. Come for daddy, Taniece. Right fucking now." As soon as those words left his mouth, I was coming and squirting all over his dick and stomach.

"Baby, I'm cumming. Cum with me. Please, daddy. Cum with me!" I screamed in sheer pleasure.

"Daddy cumming with you, baby. Fuck!" He growled while biting his lip hard. I guess it felt too good because he never pulled out.

A few seconds later, it was over and the both of us were

breathing hard. Instead of pulling out and moving off me, Noah looked at me and softly kissed me on my lips. He then wrapped his arms around me and snuggled himself between my head and neck. I honestly didn't mind because I was comfortable as fuck.

I was tired but my mind wandered off before sleep could claim me for the night. Thinking of how my sister and other females made sex sound, it was everything they said any more. I didn't hurt if you did it with someone you had actual feelings for. Which is why it was so special with Noah. I know he didn't feel the same way I did about him, but I at least knew he cared about me.

I knew when we woke up tomorrow, we were going to wake up to the bullshit. I knew he wouldn't be pleased with himself and may even regret ever touching me. That was just something I would have to swallow like a grown ass woman. Even with all the history behind why this shit is fucked up, I didn't regret a single thing that happened. I'm going to enjoy the rest of the night and live in my fantasy world before it gets fucked by reality come sun up.

Karter

Waking up out of a dead sleep, feeling groggy as fuck, I already knew that I had fucked up royally. It was bad enough that I had lied to my woman about what I was doing this morning, but to end up fucking her best friend. I was the worst kind of nigga, but I couldn't fucking help it. I love Lauriel. I loved her more than I've ever loved anyone else. But to have pussy constantly thrown at me, it was too much temptation for a nigga to handle. Honestly, there's no excuse for the bullshit I'm pulling. I knew I was wrong as fuck. I just didn't know how to stop it.

A part of me knew what Jream was up to every time she would hit me up to meet her somewhere. I didn't want my baby to find out about what we'd done behind her back, so I kept meeting her every time she called or texted.

Laying in this bed, Jream had her head on my chest, her arm and leg thrown over my body. Looking down at her, she looked so beautiful and peaceful. Like she was getting the best sleep in her life. Watching her sleep, one wouldn't be able to tell how manipulative and deceitful she could really be. Moving her body off of mine, I get out of the bed to get dressed and get out of here. I didn't know exactly what time it was, but I knew it was getting late. I went to grab my phone, but I noticed it didn't light up. It was off. This motherfucker turned my phone off.

"Jream! Get up!" She started feeling around the bed like she was looking for me and when she didn't find me, she opened her eyes. He looked in my direction and her eyes roamed down to my dick. I hadn't had the chance to find my damn clothes.

"Hey, baby." She smiled brightly.

"I'm not your baby." She frowned at my tone. "Why did you turn my phone off?"

She rolled her eyes as I asked my question. "Lauriel was calling nonstop. I just didn't want anything to get in the way of our time together." For the first time since all this shit got started, I looked at Jream. I actually looked at her. She was gorgeous to me. Spoiled as fuck and had no drive nor ambition whatsoever but she was still beautiful. Jream and Lauriel were both amazingly beautiful women. Both for different reasons. Lauriel had both superficial and inner beauty. She was hard working, caring, loving and overly ambitious. Jream, on the other hand, had superficial beauty and a slight bit of inner beauty. I could tell she wanted to cater to me in every way possible. She wanted to be at my beck and call. As much as I liked the idea of that, did I really want that?

Or did I want the woman that was going to push me to my greatest potential and not my greatest tax bracket. I can't even front and say that I didn't enjoy the pussy Jream put on me last night. Was it better than Lauriel's? I wouldn't necessarily say that, but it came damn close. Her head game had even gotten better.

"Look, Jream, you know the deal between us. You've been blackmailing a nigga just to get some dick. I'm your best friend's man. You don't think this shit is wrong as fuck?" I only asked that question to get her answer. I needed to see where her head was.

For the first time, I think I saw a slight bit of remorse on her face. Just as fast as it came, it went.

"No, it's not wrong," she said seriously. "I've wanted you before I knew you were my best friend's boyfriend.

Yes, I know this isn't the most ideal situation, but you can't tell me that you don't feel anything when you're with me."

She got out of the bed naked as the day she was born and walked closer to me. Watching her walk in my direction, I couldn't help but admire her sexy ass body. Her breasts bounced as she walked to me, pressing her body up against mine, chest to chest, my dick pressing up against her stomach. I looked down at her to stare in her eyes.

"Karter, I know in the beginning it was easy to hate me. I made it seem like I would make your life hell. I just want what I deserve."

"Don't you have a man already?"

She scoffed at what I asked. "No, I don't have man. I have a boyfriend. A man would be providing for his family and not bitching at the money that is spent. I deserve a man that wants me to have the best of everything and worships the ground I walk on. Karter, I deserve you."

I heard everything she said. I agreed to a certain extent, but then again, I didn't.

"What about wanting something for yourself? You want me to want you so bad, give me something to want.

147

Yeah, Jream, you're beautiful, there's no doubt about it. But you need more than beauty to get through this life." She looked away, not trying to hear what I had to say.

"Do you know why I fell in love with Lauriel?"

Jream stopped me from speaking before I could finish.

"You're not in love with that bitch. You just fucked me to sleep this morning and now you claim to be in love with her."

I sighed heavily. "Despite what happened last night, I am in love with Lauriel. I'm a fucked up ass nigga for even allowing this shit to go down." I gently pushed her away from me. I knew I needed to get the fuck from around here. I shouldn't have been here in the first place.

I turned around to grab my clothes to take a quick shower and head back to Lauriel's place. Jream started pulling at my arm to stop me.

"No, don't go. At least give me a chance. That's all I need, a chance to show you that I'm the woman for you." Deciding to play along with her game for now, I decided to tell her what she wanted to hear.

"Alright, baby. I'll give you a chance. But you have to

listen to me." I stared in her eyes so she could know just how serious I am. "You can't go running your mouth because shit is not going your way. If you want me to walk away from my woman, you're going to be patient and let me handle this like I need to."

Jream was hanging on to every word like a dog hangs on to a bone. I had zero intentions on leaving Lauriel, but she didn't need to know that. In my head, I could have the best of both worlds. Plus, by telling Jream whatever she needed to hear, I knew I she would be less likely to rat me out. Baby girl jumped in my arms and kissed all over my face. I couldn't help but laugh. She started kissing me and moaning as soon as our lips met.

"Fuck me, Karter. Fuck me hard!" That shit was turning me the fuck on. As soon as I put her down on the bed, she pulled out a condom and put it on my dick with her mouth.

Shit, I was already in trouble with my baby, I might as well prolong the shit as much as I could and get some fire pussy in the meantime.

*

After giving Jream what she wanted one more time, I jumped in the shower and finally made my way to Lauriel's house. Looking at the dashboard, I saw it was close to eleven o'clock in the morning. I just knew when I got inside, she was going to be pissed. Especially since she couldn't get in touch with me. When I pulled up to her townhouse, I saw her car there so I knew she was home. I said a silent prayer and got out the car, preparing myself for the wrath that's coming my way. I put my key in the lock and pushed the door open. I looked in the living room and she was sitting on the sofa in her robe with a glass of wine in her hand.

Before I could utter a word, she said, "Where have you been?"

"Baby, I told you. I had to go pick up my teammate after he got into with his girl. I drove him around to find a hotel and I ended up falling asleep on the sofa in his suite." That was the best I could come up with, but I had to admit, that shit was pretty damn good.

"Well, why didn't you answer the phone? I called you after you had been gone for more than an hour. I was worried sick about your ass." I could see the worry lines in her face and I felt like shit for making her feel that. I couldn't incriminate myself though. I had to keep this lie going because I refused to this shit to ruin what I had going on.

"My phone must have died after I fell asleep. Plus, I forgot my charger here, bae. I have to get a new one to keep in my car." She seemed to be buying the bullshit I was giving to her.

She reached up to hug me, and I gladly accepted.

"I'm sorry if I came off accusatory. I was just really worried about you, baby. When you didn't answer your phone, I thought the worst. Shit also didn't help after the words that were exchanged between me and Jream." I hope she didn't feel me tense up, but I did. What the fuck was she talking about.

"Words exchanged between you and Jream? What did that have to do with me?" She looked away before she answered me; she was making my ass nervous. I swear to God, if Jream said something to mess my shit up, I was fucking her world up.

"What did she say, Lauriel?"

"When we were out last night, I kind of was getting some shit off my chest. I told them how you've been distant lately and I was worried about us. She basically said that maybe you were acting like that because you would be going on the road soon and you didn't want to feel like you were settling with me."

"The fuck? How am I settling with you?"

She looked down when she said, "Because you have so many beautiful women throwing themselves at you. You may feel like you're settling by being with me." So that's how Jream wanted to play this shit.

I placed my hands gently around Lauriel's face and said, "Baby, I could never be settling with you. You're the complete package. You're all I could want in a woman. I love your fine ass, girl. Don't ever doubt my love or faithfulness to you." Without waiting for a response from her, I kissed her long and hard on the lips. I needed her to feel the love I had for her through this kiss.

"I'm sorry, baby. I shouldn't be listening to anyone else about my man, especially people that don't even know my man."

"Damn straight. And the next time you feel any kind of way about me and what we have going on, you come to me. Not your miserable ass best friend that doesn't even like herself." I laid that shit on thick. For a second she looked at me skeptically, but she then agreed. I gently gave her one last kiss before I went to go take another shower, so I could lay up with my baby all day.

I felt guilty as fuck for making her feel like she was wrong for going to her friend about us, but I had to. Like I said before, I couldn't have her finding out about the shit I had going on. Between dealing with my agents and the Saints front office going over my contract, making time for Lauriel and trying to fit Jream's ass in there somewhere, I was stretched thin. I keep saying I love my girl, but I was looking like a fuck up.

Part of me couldn't believe how Jream tried to play it by planting that seed in my baby's head but another part of me could. The fucking girl was manipulative as fuck. She had her eyes on the prize and that prize was me. She'd stop at nothing to get what she wanted and I was going to watch and see just how far she'd go. I was coming out on top in the end. As long as I gave her the hope she longed for, she was going to keep this shit under wraps. She just didn't know, she was going to be the biggest fool in the end. I was never leaving my baby for her, but I was going to enjoy her thinking that I would.

Noah

That same morning

Stirring in my sleep, the sunlight that was peeking through the window was blinding me. I must have fallen asleep on the sofa because we had those blackout curtains in our room. Then again, I couldn't be on the sofa because our sofa wasn't this fucking comfortable.

Finally peeling my eyes open, I realize I'm in unfamiliar surroundings. Sitting up to gather myself, I noticed there's a body next to me. Before I could figure out what the fuck is going on, Taniece, beautiful ass Taniece, the same girl that's invaded my thoughts for a while now, was staring directly at me.

"Good morning, Noah," she said in her soft voice.

"Uh, Good morning."

I didn't want to come off as standoffish but fuck, I didn't know what was going on. Why the fuck was I here, much less in the bed with this girl? Moving to get out the bed, I pull the covers back and saw I was completely naked.

"What the fuck?" At this moment, I couldn't hide my confusion. "T, did we? Tell me we didn't, man. Tell me, Taniece." I looked at her and saw the hurt and remorse written on her face. I hated to see her like that, but I needed answers.

"You don't remember anything that happened last night?" She asked timidly.

I took time to think about the question she just asked me. I honestly don't remember much except talking Jream. She pissed me the fuck off when she told me that she wasn't coming home because she had to be there for Taniece. For one, I knew that they all were friends, but if Taniece was going through something, why not call her sister? Then for her to block my number took me over the edge. I was at my breaking point with this fuck ass relationship and I didn't know what to do next. I started drinking some Hennessy and thinking about my next move. After trying to call her all night long, I got up off my ass and made my way to T's house. I didn't remember shit else after that.

"All I really remember is coming over here looking for

Jream. She obviously wasn't here."

Sighing heavily, she said, "You came over here at almost four o'clock this morning looking for Jream. I had no idea why you thought she would be here. You thought I was lying to you. After it was determined she wasn't here, you sat on the sofa and talked about how you were feeling. Then you got up to leave, told me thank you for listening, you hugged me and we kissed." Looking down at her bed and body, she said, "Then we ended up here."

Shocked was an understatement for how I felt. Don't get me wrong, I was sexually attracted to Taniece, but I was a faithful nigga. I didn't give any other woman my time nor attention. Shit, trying to keep Jream happy was a fucking full-time job with overtime. I couldn't believe I allowed myself to take it there with her. I was pissed with myself.

"I'm sorry, T. I honestly don't remember all that happened, but I know this wasn't supposed to happen." I got up to find my clothes so I could leave. I hated feeling like I took advantage of my friend. Taniece was quietly watching my every move. She didn't say a word, but I could see the questions in her face.

From the corner of my eye, I could see she was getting out the bed. I assumed to find her clothes. I couldn't help but to stare at her sexy ass body as she glided across the room.

"Look, Noah," she said as she walked up to me. "I know last night wasn't planned, but I need you to know that I don't regret it whatsoever. I had been saving myself all this time for that special person. I just never knew it would be you." She reached up to caress my face. I knew she was trying to calm the nerves I had about feeling like I used her ,but all she did was make another light bulb go off in my head.

"Did you just say you had been saving yourself?" She looked away when I said that. Using my hand to pull her face to me, to make her look me in the eyes, I said, "Taniece, you gave me your virginity?" I damn near yelled when I said it. Nodding her head in response, I felt even worse than I did before.

"Fuck, Fuck, Fuck, Fuck!" If I wasn't pissed before, I was definitely pissed now. How the fuck did I let shit get so out of hand? I only came over here looking for my fucking girlfriend and I ended up sleeping with her friend.

Then I thought about it. I came over here looking for my girlfriend, and her ass wasn't even fucking here. So, if she wasn't where she said she was going to be then where the fuck was she?

Looking at the clock on her nightstand, I saw that it was right at ten o'clock in the morning. I finally gathered all my shit. Now I had to get the fuck out of here and get my ass home.

"Taniece, I know you and I have to talk about last night, but I don't have the time right now. I promise, I'll come back soon so we can talk and hash all this shit out." I reached down to kiss her on the forehead.

"I understand. Don't be too hard on yourself, Noah. You didn't come over here with the intention to have sex with me. Shit just happened. Don't worry, this stays between us." With that said, she reached up and kissed my cheek. I swear I felt the electricity coming from her kiss. I wanted to address what I was feeling, but I just didn't have the time right now.

I got in my car, ready to deal with the hurricane I knew I had coming at home. I checked my phone and saw I had no missed calls or text messages. I had so many questions running through my head. In this moment, nothing added up to me. I knew I was fucked up for what happened last night, but Jream had a lot of fucking explaining to do. Why the fuck wasn't she at Taniece's house when she told me that's where she would be? Did she think I was that stupid that I would just let the whole night go by without trying to find her ass. She put me on the fucking block list with no regard for shit. What if something happened to me or worse, something happened to NyJae? Granted, I understood he was with my parents, but I didn't give a fuck.

Then, the shit that happened with me and T last night fucked with me heavy. I knew that she had been on my mind for a while now. I'm guilty to the fact that when I've been having sex with Jream, I'm thinking about Taniece. My attraction to her had intensified over the years and it had nothing to do with how beautiful she was. I was attracted to her personality, her drive, her ambition. She had a fire behind her eyes that I found sexier than her actual physique. She was the kind of woman that made a man want to do better. She made a man want to succeed at everything he set his mind to just so she could be proud.

That's exactly how Jream used to make me feel. My woman use to make me feel so proud to be her man. She made me feel like I could do no wrong in her eyes. She once used to stare at me in adoration. Shit like that make a nigga chest poke out. When your woman trusts you with her lively hood. When I started my business and had to pour all my resources into it, that trust inside of her dwindled. It hurt me that she no longer looked at me like that. Jream never understood, we weren't broke, we just weren't as comfortable as we use to be.

I just needed her to trust me. Trust that I would put us back in that position to be more than comfortable. The plans that I had and the hard work I was putting in, Jream wouldn't have to lift another finger in her life. Shit was coming together, she just didn't know. She just needed to trust me. In my heart, I knew that ship had sailed long time ago. My girlfriend no longer trusted me, but my friend trusted me with her mind, body and soul. Part of me feels honored that Taniece gave me such a gift, but another part of me wishes she wouldn't have. Even with all that I knew and felt about her, I still had no intention to take her virginity. She was my friend before anything, I would never take advantage of her. She didn't deserve to be treated like a quick fuck, and that's how I felt like I treated her. I guess with all the shit I had going on, talking to her made me want her, and I just allowed myself to have her. It was mind boggling that she didn't stop me. Why didn't she stop me?

I finally made it home with all this shit running through my mind. I needed a minute to get my shit together.

Jumping out the car, I rush inside. "Jream!" I look all over the house, constantly screaming her name. This motherfucker still wasn't home. I didn't know if I should be pissed or worried. I was pissed because she lied about her whereabouts and worried because I didn't know if she was alright. It made no sense to try and call her because none of my calls would go through. The only thing I could think of was to call Lauriel. She was the last person she was with last night.

Just went I about to press her name to call her, I hear Jream's keys unlocking the door. She walked in the door wearing that same stupid outfit she had on last night without a care in the world. She didn't even bother to say anything to me. Walked right pass me on her way to the bathroom. Now that I know she was ok, I was no longer worried. I was angry. I ran behind her and damn near knocked the hinges off that bathroom door.

WHAM!

"What the fuck is wrong with you?" She yelled in my face.

"No, what the fuck is wrong with you? You hung up in my face last night then blocked me." She waved her hand dismissively.

"I didn't feel like arguing with you, Noah. You got mad because I chose to be there for my girl rather than lay up under your ass all day. Get over it." I had never in my life wanted to put my hands on a woman, but I wanted to fuck her ass up right now.

I walked away calmly and sat on the edge of the bed.

163

The fact that she was standing in front of me lying to my face was enough for me to start breaking shit in this motherfucker. I needed to calm my nerves before I did something I was going to regret.

"Jream, where were you last night?" I asked in the calmest tone I could muster.

She rolled her eyes and said, "I told you I stayed by Taniece's house. She was going through it with her dude and she needed me to be there for her." That lie just rolled off her tongue with no regret nor remorse.

"You sure?" She just looked at me. "Because I find it funny that you were nowhere near Taniece's house when I went there looking for you four o'clock this morning."

She looked away but said nothing.

"Nah, don't get quiet now. Speak up. Where the fuck were you?" I usually didn't speak to her like this, but I was beyond sick of her shit.

"The fuck were you doing? Spying on me? You don't trust me?" I looked at her incredulously.

"Bitch, I know you playing with me. I just know this is a joke," I said while shaking my head. I walked up to her so we could be face to face, damn near nose to nose.

"Bitch?" She shrieked.

"Jream, I see you take me as a game to play with. See, you think shit sweet. I've been letting you walk around this motherfucker getting away with murder. Why? Because I love you, but that shit is dwindling fast. Now you got me fucked up. A nigga is beyond tired of your trifling ass. Now either you tell me where you were, or I'm gonna start taking all your shit and throwing it outside."

In the five years that she and I have been together, I have never threatened to leave her, much less put her out. Even though shit had gotten bad over the last few years, it had never gotten that bad where I wanted us to break up. I was finally at that point.

"So, you're going to put me and my son out because you think I'm lying." She paused for a second. "I told you where I was. If you don't believe me, that's on you."

"Let's clear up two things. One, I would never put my son out. He will stay with me while you go back wherever the fuck you came from. Two, I don't think you were lying, I know you were lying. Did you not hear me say that I went

165

to that girl's house looking for you? I called her a liar when she told me you weren't there. She looked at me like a fucking fool because she had no clue that you were supposed to be there."

I took a minute to breathe and try to calm myself once again.

"Now, I'm going to ask you one more time. Where the fuck were you?"

"I doesn't matter how many times you ask me, my answer won't change. How do you know I didn't get there after you left? I had you blocked so there was no way for you to contact me."

I was pissed off that I couldn't tell her why I knew she never even showed up there, so I had to play my part and bite my tongue.

"You know what, fuck this and fuck you. I don't need this shit, nor do I deserve it. Keep the apartment, I don't give a fuck."

I didn't even bother grabbing anything, I just picked up my keys and walked out of the apartment. I didn't have time to deal with Jream and her bullshit. It was always some shit with her. For her to blatantly lie to my face was a final straw for me. I couldn't and wouldn't take this shit anymore. I would always be there for Nyjae, but his mama could kick rocks with open toe shoes.

Jumping in my car, I drove to the only place I knew I'd find refuge. My parent's house. My pops is my best friend. I would go to him and talk to him about anything under the sun and I knew he would never judge me. Pulling in my parent driveway, I only saw Pop's car, making me assume my mama was out and about. I walked to the door and unlocked it to find Pops laid out in his recliner asleep.

"Wake up, old man," I said as I slapped the side of his chair.

He jumped up out his sleep looking crazy. "Boy, you gon' make me fuck you up."

"Your old ass ain't gon' do shit." We both started laughing. I was more comfortable to talk freely around him. He didn't care if I cursed. My mama didn't play that shit. She'd fuck me up in a heartbeat.

"Where's ma and Nyjae?"

"Your mama took him to the store with her. That lil

nigga been bouncing around all day and he wore my ass out." I knew my son was a handful. He had the energy of six toddlers and he didn't mind showing it.

"Let me find out Nyjae giving you a run for your money."

"I'm too old for this shit, Noah. You know I love my grandson, but his mama drops him off over whenever her ass itch too much. Does she ever spend time with him?"

I hesitated before answering him. I knew Jream loved Nyjae. I didn't have a doubt about that. She just didn't know how not to make it all about her. When Nyjae was born, she was in full mommy mode. It was beautiful to watch. Problem is, that shit only lasted for a couple weeks. It was like it clicked in her head, it was no longer about her anymore. So, she started doing the bare minimum. When she felt like her job was done for the day, she would drop my son off to whomever would watch him.

"I know, Pop. I'm sorry this shit is happening. I hate that she thinks it's cool to just leave him here like you guys don't have a life. As soon as I could get my schedule on track, I'll be able to keep him more." I sighed heavily.

"What's going on, son? What's the problem?" My father said, looking at me intently.

I sat there and told my father everything that happened. From me looking for Jream, to her lying about her whereabouts, to me sleeping with Taniece. After I finished talking to him, I felt like the weight of the world had been lifted off my shoulders. Pops looked shocked by everything I laid on him.

"Damn, son. You laid a lot on me. Sounds to me like both of ya'll fucked up royaly."

"Pop, I know I made a mistake last night. I'm not negating that. But this shit with Jream has been going on long before the one mistake I made last night."

"True, but that doesn't make you right for what you did nor how you did it." Leave it to my father to put me in my place no matter how bad I had been wronged.

"You right, but I can't do this shit anymore. I have exhausted all efforts to make this shit work, but I'm done. I watched for years while you catered to Ma and gave her everything she could want or need." My father looked at me like he was waiting for me to say more.

"Yes, but your mother was also deserving of everything I ever did for her." He paused for a minute. Sighing, he said, "Son, I know you two have had a rough patch over the years, but are you sure you're done?"

I sat and thought about it for a while. Did I really want to walk away from the woman I once loved more than life itself? The answer was becoming easier every day. If I was being honest with myself, Jream had left me a long time ago. Her body was physically in the same apartment as me, but her heart had been walked out the door.

"Pop, I love Jream. I really do. I was planning to propose to her and everything but shit just hasn't been right in a very long time. I never wanted to admit it to myself, but now I have to."

As soon as those words left my mouth I heard, "Thank you, Jesus. It's about time."

My mother was walking into the living room caring my Baby boy on her hip.

"Daddy!!!" He jumped out of her arms and ran to me. I loved his reaction every time he saw me. It made me feel proud to be his daddy.

"Hey, little man." I kissed the top of his head. He was content with being in my arms and I was content holding him. After the night and morning I had, I was happy to have the one person that loved me despite every flaw I had.

My mother walked over and kissed me on my forehead.

"Hey, ma."

"Hey, baby. Now what is this I hear about you leaving your little girlfriend."

I laughed at my mother's question. I wouldn't necessarily say that my mother didn't like Jream, she just didn't tolerate her behavior. Let's not forget, she hated how she treated me. I never would tell my mother about the shit that went on in our relationship but often times, Jream was bold enough to pull her foul moves of inconsideration in front of my mother and piss her completely off.

"We can talk about this later, ma, I just want to go in my old room and put my son down for his nap." I could see my father giving her the eye, basically telling her to let me be and I appreciated it. I wouldn't mind talking to her later on but right now, a nigga just needed to clear his head and get some rest.

Going upstairs, to my room. I pull the covers back and turn the tv on cartoons so we could get comfortable and chill. I knew I'd have to deal with all the shit that was going on later, but right now, I didn't have the patience. I just wanted to spend some much-needed time with my son.

Lauriel

Watching Karter walk away to go take his shower, a lot of shit played in my head. When I couldn't get in touch with him last night, I'm not even gonna lie, I thought the worst. I knew that he told me that he had to go get his homeboy because he got into it with his girl, but it shouldn't have taken that fucking long. I was pissed off that I was sitting in this house just watching the clock. Every minute that passed, I was getting more and more angry. I was trying to control my anger so much so, I called my mother to calm me down.

"Lauriel, girl, do you see what time it is? Are you alright?" I hadn't even paid attention to the fact that it was six am.

"I'm sorry, ma, but I'm so mad. Do you know Karter left out of here after three to go help his teammate and hasn't been back since?" I was fuming.

"Did you try calling him?" She asked.

"Did I try?" I said in my Soulja Boy voice. "Ma, I called that man almost twenty times, no answer."

"First of all, you need to calm down. Maybe he got sidetracked with his friend. Leave that man alone, he will come home soon." My mama was aggravating me because she was way too calm. I needed her to have some kind of turn up about her then calm me down. I know I sounded stupid.

"Man, I should have called my Teeny Boo." My mama started laughing when I said that.

"Yea, you call your Teeny Boo and she would have had you ready to burn that man house down." I laughed because I knew she was right. I felt a little bit better after talking to my mama. I just needed someone to talk to me and take my mind off things.

"He'll be home soon, baby. Call me later on and tell me what the hell he said about having you worry."

After I got off the phone with my mama, I just sat on the sofa listening to music and sipping wine. My mind was too wound up to sleep. Now that he was home and safe, my mind was slightly at ease. I just couldn't shake the feeling that I was being lied to. I had no proof but something deep in my stomach was bugging the hell out of me.

I'm not sure what it was, but I knew if there was something I needed to know, it would come to light sooner or later. I knew I shouldn't have been listening to what Jream said. Her ass was miserable and wanted me to be miserable right along with her. But I wondered if there was some truth to it. God forbid, if Karter was cheating on me, I want to kill him. I'd been too good of a woman to deserve that. For now, I'm not going to concern myself with the what ifs of the world. I'm just going to focus on the right now. And right now, my fine ass man was home and I wanted him.

I walked in the bedroom and I heard the shower going. I decided that I was going to join my baby. Taking off my robe, I walked in the bathroom. The steam was making the shower door and mirror fog up. I walked to the shower door and opened it, only to be met with surprise expression from Karter.

"Baby, I just wanted to take a quick shower and get in the bed to go back to sleep. I got you later, baby." With that, he closed the door.

What the fuck was that? Feeling rejected, I walked back out to the room to climb in my bed. I rarely laid in the bed naked, but I wanted to see what he was going to do when he noticed I was.

About fifteen minutes later, Karter finally emerged from the bathroom with a towel wrapped around his waist. I smelled his body wash as soon as he came in the room and he smelled damn good. I was horny and I needed my man to take care of me. After he dried his body off, he threw the towel back in the bathroom and came over to climb in the bed. He reached over to kiss me on the forehead, then he turn his back to me and got comfortable under the covers.

I was hurt. It was like he didn't even notice me. In the six months we've been together, he's never rejected me. If he wasn't accepting my advances, he was making advances of his own. He didn't even turn over to hold me. I heard his breathing pattern change which meant he had fallen asleep. Well, I'm glad he could sleep so peacefully because once again, I couldn't get a wink of sleep. This shit was going to bother me until I found out what was going on.

*

Football season was in full swing and today was his first game of the season. It was an away game in Cleveland. We had been talking about finding time to go visit his family so that I could meet them. What better time than to go during a game.

It had been a few months since we had hit our rough patch. After the night he stayed out all night and him rejecting me that same morning, I felt like Karter and I needed to sit down and have a long conversation. I went to him and told him how I was feeling and how he made me felt. While I talked to him, he listened intently. Karter gave me his undivided attention. When I was through talking, he apologized and told me with him having so much going on, he didn't realize he made me feel like he had. He held me tightly and told me that he going to do better and be a better man to me.

After we had that conversation, any doubt or uneasiness I had flew out the window. I felt like I was looking at the man I had fallen in love with. Whatever had taken place prior to our talk, no longer matter. Karter and I were back tight like before and I was enjoying our flourishing relationship. We put our all into loving each other and I was the happiest I had been in my whole life. Even when he went to minicamp, he made as much time as he could to talk to me. They had to stick to a very rigorous schedule. If he didn't have the time to call and check in, he would text me to let me know he missed me and he loved me. I appreciated how he catered to nurturing our relationship.

I wouldn't really say we had any sore spots. The only thing that aggravates me is how fucking stingy he is with his phone. He's always on it and when he puts it down, he places it face down. For most women, that would be a major red flag. I just chose to ignore it. I felt in my heart if Karter is doing me dirty in any kind of way, I would find out. I wanted to enjoy what our love had become. I didn't want to go around snooping, come up with nothing and end up looking stupid. I didn't want him to think I didn't trust him. Karter was granted my full trust until he gave me a reason not to trust him.

"Lauriel, you ready to go to the stadium, baby girl?" I heard Karter's mom, Karen, yell from downstairs.

"Yes, ma'am, I'm on my way down now."

Karter and I had come down Friday before his game so I could meet his immediate family. He had a pretty decent size family. His parents got a divorce some years ago so I ended up meeting his mother, Karen, stepfather, Emory and his father, Brent. Karter had three brothers, Kaine, Kendall, Karic, and a sister named Kenari. Kaine was the oldest at thirty-five, Kendall was thirty-three, Karic was thirty-two. He and Kendall were eleven months apart. Lastly, Karter was twenty-eight and Kenari was twenty-six. Karter loved all his brothers and sisters, but he worshiped the ground Kenari walked on. I understood it because I felt the exact same way about my sister. She and I had talked on the phone before I met her and I loved her personality.

When we got to the hotel, Ms. Karen acted a plum fool. She cursed Karter's ass out from sun up to sun down. She told him we better have our asses at her house with our luggage or she was going to beat his ass. I was weak. With his tail tucked between his legs, we checked out of the hotel and made our way to the beautiful mini mansion Karter bought for his parents his third year in the league. I swear, their house was my dream home. From the long driveway to the beautiful six bedrooms that had their own personal décor. Their kitchen was like the ones in the movie. And don't get me started on the pool area. I needed all this in my life and I couldn't wait until I could make it happen for myself.

The first night there, Ms. Karen had made a delicious dinner. She wanted us to sit around the table, catch up and get to know each other. I swear, all Karter's brothers were fools. Only his brother, Kaine, had a girlfriend and she was in attendance also. Kenari and Ms. Karen couldn't stand the girl. It was so bad, I couldn't even remember what her name was. All they kept calling her was heffa. She seemed like the stuck-up kind. While I was throwing down on them collard greens, baked chicken, baked macaroni and cheese, mashed potatoes and sweet potato pie, she was turning up her nose at it. When dinner was over, all the women decided to help clear the table and start the dishes, but she decided to sit up under Kaine. That burnt Karen up and she didn't hide her dislike.

On Saturday, Karter had to go meet his team at their hotel. I was planning on going back to the hotel that night, but his mother wouldn't hear of it. She made it a point to let me know my ass better not leave her house. I could clearly see why Karter gravitated to my mother the way he did. She was just as loving and welcoming as his mother. They went out of their way to make others feel comfortable. I was glad I had finally had the opportunity to meet his family.

Looking in the mirror, I was admiring my attire for the game today. I was wearing a black female fitted Saints Jersey with Karter's number on the back. Instead of it saying "Montegue", it said "Mrs. Montegue." I was rocking some distress dark denim jeans and some custom Saints Jordan's that I created myself. I decided to wear my hair bone straight over one shoulder so the name on my jersey could be seen at all times. I grabbed my cell phone and my crossbody and was ready to go cheer my baby on. When I made it downstairs, his parents looked at me funny.

"What?" I was trying to find out what was wrong.

Mr. Emory looked at Ms. Karen and said, "Baby, why didn't you rep your man like Lauriel repping Karter today?" I started laughing.

"You want me to come to court wearing a t-shirt with your face on it? You got it, baby," Ms. Karen clowned. Mr. Emory was a criminal defense attorney with an extremely high success rate.

"No, that's ok, baby. You cheer me on damn good when I get home from court." Ms. Karen blushed hard as hell. They were such a beautiful couple. I hoped that if Karter and I lasted that long, we'd be just as in love or even more in love than his parents.

"Girl, come on. Let's get out of here so we can beat the traffic." We jumped in Mr. Emory's black Infinity truck and made our way to the stadium. Along the way, I admired the sites of the city. Cleveland was a beautiful city. I wouldn't mind coming here again really soon.

Luckily, the traffic wasn't as bad as we expected so we made it there in no time. I was so excited to cheer my man on. I knew he wouldn't be able to see me or hear me, but he knew I was there.

"Lauriel, is there anything special we can get for you for the picnic today?" Karter's family was throwing him a first game picnic for after the game. His whole family wanted to meet his new girlfriend and celebrate after the game. Win, Lose or Draw, Karter's family supported him. It was a beautiful thing.

"No, ma'am. Whatever you guys have is good with me." I wasn't a picky person so I was good with whatever.

"Girl, I done told you about that ma'am business. You better learn how to call me Karen."

"I'm sorry. My mama taught my sister and I, anybody that was older than you was Ms. or Mr., Sir or Ma'am. I wasn't about to get popped in the mouth for disrespecting my mama." They both started laughing.

"I know that's right. I understand, baby. I taught my kids the exact same thing. I didn't play that shit." She paused in thought. "The only child that gave me hell was that damn Kaine. Normally they say your first child is your best child. The lies they tell. Kaine gave my ass the blues for the longest. And his father never wanted me to beat his ass. Until I met Emory. Kenari had just made one, their father and my divorce had just been finalized. He and I started dating and he loved all my children, but that damn Kaine gave us a run for our money. Now Emory would never lay a finger on any of my children, but he kept telling me I needed to beat his lil ass or I would always have a problem." She laughed at the thought. "Girl, one day, I had had enough. All my kids were well-mannered, polite and listened to everything I said. He just refused to do right. So, he called himself disrespecting me and I wore his little nine-year-old ass out. I could no longer take it. He was crying and snotting everywhere. He got so mad, he called himself calling his daddy on me. Brent called me trying to go off on me about his son, and I cursed his ass out. Told him he needed to get his son in check or I was sending Kaine to him on the first thing smoking. Well, his ass didn't want that. He barely wanted to get the kids on his scheduled days. Needless to say, he finally got that ass in check and I didn't have another problem out of him."

Ms. Karen was so real and honest. I really enjoyed listening to the stories she shared about her family and her children. My favorites were about Karter and Kenari and how sneaky they used to be. They would do shit, cover for the other and wouldn't say a word. If one got in trouble, they both did. There was no ratting out the other.

We got out of the car and made our way up to the skybox. This was my first time at a professional football game. I was super excited. When we walked inside, we were greeted by the rest of his family, including his biological daddy. They all greeted me and we started enjoying all the amenities in the skybox.

About an hour later, the game started and the Saints were winning, 14-0. My man had scored both touchdowns. I was screaming my ass off, making a complete fool of myself. Everybody was laughing at me, but I didn't care. I was here to cheer my man on. He had worked so hard to stay in shape, studying his playbook and scheduling extra practices. He deserved every bit of recognition he was receiving. During halftime, I grabbed a bottle of water and sat my ass down to catch my breath. I pulled out my phone to make sure I hadn't missed any important emails or phone calls. When I saw that I hadn't,

I decide to waste some time on IG until halftime was over.

As soon the app loaded, All Tea, All Day popped up and they were talking about Karter. Apparently, a post was made about Karter. Some girl was claiming to be his girlfriend. She was saying how she was sad she was missing his first game and she couldn't wait 'til he came home so they could celebrate their win. The worse part of it all, my name was plastered on this shit, saying that I was supposed to be his girlfriend so obviously, there was trouble in paradise.

"I was really hoping I got to you before you saw it," Kenari said over my shoulder. I assume she was looking at my phone behind me.

I was honestly speechless. This is the shit I was worried about when we first decided to go public with our relationship. I didn't have time for this bullshit. I was a self-made businesswoman. I had too much going for myself to deal with scandal like this whether it's real or false.

"Lauriel, I hope you don't feed into this bullshit. My brother hasn't been serious with a woman in a long ass time. He wouldn't give none of these thirsty ass hoes the times of day," Kenari said, trying to make me feel better.

"I hear what you're saying. I really do, but I'm not going to feel better until I talk to Karter."

"You're really going to even take this shit to him? This is social media. You have to believe none of what you see and only half of what you hear. Girl, you are so much better than this. Ignore that shit." I understood what she was saying. I really did. But still, why did it come up now after all this time? This shit was real coincidental. All this time, I hadn't dealt with anything like this. Why now?

For the remainder of the game, I chilled in my spot and just observed. I was too aggravated to continue cheering him on feeling like I felt. I was asked numerous times was I ok but as comfortable as his family had made me, I wasn't that comfortable telling them how I felt.

Feeling my phone vibrate, I checked to see who it was.

Taniece: Bitch, have you been on IG today?

Duchess: Cousin, am I beating your man's ass? Do I need to call my mama? You know how we coming behind you.

Keshyra: Do we even know if this is real before we decide to beat Karter's ass?

Duchess: Ugh, I swear. Bitch, you'd think Teedy Vera had you. You too fucking calm for me. I need you to act like Teeny Boo child for once Key.

Taniece: Shut up, Duch! I need my sister to answer us or else, I'm on the first thing smoking to Cleveland.

Duchess: And bitch, you know I'm riding shot gun!

Keshyra: Pick me up on the way.

I was weak laughing at our group message. I hurriedly texted them to tell them I saw the post and I was ok. I would call them on a conference call after I talked to Karter. The only person I realized hadn't checked on me was my best friend. Granted, Jream and I's relationship took a drastic turn. We barely spoke and when we did, it was dry as hell. I really only called to check on my godson. Now that she and Noah were on bad terms, she barely had him. I still didn't know what that was about. She never enlightened me. Instead of waiting to see if she would reach out to me, I decided to reach out to her first. Pulling out my phone, I sent a text.

Me: Hey, best. I know you probably saw that post on IG. You wasn't gonna check on your bestie?

About five minutes later, I received a response.

Jream: I don't know why you expected me to check on you. Every time I say anything about your precious Karter, you catch an attitude. I hate to say it but I told you so.

Me: Damn, Jream. Can't you be considerate for once? Do you always have to kick a bitch while she's down? And we don't really know if anything happened. But fuck, check on me.

Jream: If we don't know if anything happened, what am I checking on you for?

Instead of responding, I decided to just ignore her petty ass. She was beyond miserable and I refused to be miserable with her. I had enough on my mind and I didn't need her adding to it.

I was so thankful when this game was over. Even though I was happy they won, I just wanted to get back to the house and get through this party. It didn't make sense to wait on Karter because he had to shower, change and he had pre game interviews. The rest of us had jumped in our cars and made our way to the house. Ms. Karen had gotten a decorator to create a theme for a Saints party. She even got a *Congratulations* cake. I guess she knew they were going to win.

An hour or two after the party was in full swing, Karter had finally arrived.

"Ayyyye!!!" Everyone cheered as soon as he came in the house. He was receiving hugs and kisses from all his family. There was a lot of family he hadn't seen in a long time. I wanted him to enjoy his family, so I just chilled in the cut and waited until he found me.

"Girl, if you don't get your ass up and go hug your man," Ms. Karen said when she a saw me sitting down.

"I'm letting him speak to his family." She looked at him skeptically. Then, she grabbed my hand and pulled me in the kitchen.

"First of all, I need you to fix your face. Kenari told me about some post that you saw on the internet. I understand that got you in your feelings, but you're supposed to know your man. Shit like this not only happens to athletes, so you're not the only woman this can happen to. It's how you handle it that makes you different from the rest. Now, do you trust my son?"

Without hesitation, I said, "Yes." I knew I trusted Karter, but this shit just got under my skin. What woman wanted to see their man in any kind of scandal with another woman? I damn sure didn't.

"Well there you have it. You get out there and go find your man. If it's bothering you that much, address it when it's just you and him. Don't give nobody the satisfaction of seeing you sweat. These thirsty motherfuckers feed off that shit."

"You're right." She looked at me and winked.

"I know, baby girl. Now, go ahead and find that big head ass son of mines."

I laughed at her. She didn't know how much I appreciated that talk we just had. I knew I needed to get it together. I knew at some point, there was going to be some lil bitch that would try their hand at getting some attention from my baby. I just had to learn not to feed into the bullshit.

I walked out of the kitchen and started looking around

for Karter. He wasn't in the living room, nor out in the backyard. I went in the direction of the room we had been staying in while we had been here. As I got closer to the door, I heard a lot of rustling but not much else. When I opened the door, his back was turned and he had his phone up against his ear. When he started talking, it came out as a whisper.

"Why are you whispering?" He spun around like I scared the shit out of him.

"Huh?" I looked at him like he was stupid, because just like my mama said, If you can huh, you can hear.

"Why are you whispering?"

"Oh shit, I didn't even realize I was." I pulled the phone away from his ear and hung up on whoever was calling.

"Who was that?"

"That was just my coach. He was telling me I didn't have to come back until Tuesday because he knew I was spending time with my family." For some reason, I didn't believe shit he was saying. Maybe it was because of that stupid ass post from earlier that made me feel like I couldn't trust him, or maybe it was the way he was acting.

I didn't know but the shit was getting on my nerves.

"Ok." Instead of pushing the subject, I just let it go. "Congrats on the win today. You did amazing." No matter how I felt, I meant that from the heart.

"Thank you, baby. I see you came reppin' your man today. I likes," he said with a laugh.

He pulled me to him and hugged me tightly. I decided to take Ms. Karen's advice and know my man. I was letting this go for now, but I promise, if one more thing comes about, he's going to wish he never fucked with me.

Jream

"Why would you make that post on Instagram?" Karter asked in a harsh whisper.

"What are you talking about, baby?" I knew exactly what he was talking about, but I refused to admit anything.

"Cut the bullshit, Jream. As soon as I heard about the post and saw it for myself, I knew it was you." Oooh, he sounded really mad at me. I didn't care. I was mad too.

"Look, I don't know what you're talking about." I planned to continue this charade until he forgot about it.

"Why can't you just be honest? That's some fucked up shit you pulled. You knew the blogs would post that and you knew Lauriel would see it."

I rolled my eyes when he said that. Why the fuck would I care if she saw it? I wanted her to see it. I was tired of waiting for him to leave her. Shit wasn't going my way and I didn't like it. I needed him to hurry up and send her on her way so I could have my man and the lavish lifestyle I deserve. Instead of responding to him, I just remained quiet.

194

"Jream, you ain't gonna say anything?"

Before I could respond, I heard, "Why are you whispering?" I felt my anger rise once again just hearing her voice.

"Huh?" He said to her like he was scared.

"Why are you whispering?" *Beep, Beep, Beep.* The three beeps in my ear indicated that he had hung up on me. I just threw my phone on the sofa while blowing out an air of frustration. At this moment, I was out of answers. I think I was even more frustrated that Karter flipped the script on me. When this shit between us first started, I held all the cards. Telling him that if he didn't give me what I wanted, I would tell Lauriel, kept him coming back each time I called or texted him. All that changed the moment he put that dick in my life. I was fucking putty in his hands.

The next morning after we had sex, I poured my heart out by telling him he was the man I deserved. I felt like he actually listened to me. When he told me to just be patient with him, that was all I needed to hear. I didn't care about shit else but waiting on my man to make me his woman. Shit, I was already his woman, but I meant officially. I wanted the world to know I was his. It didn't even matter to me that Noah wanted nothing to do with me. I was cool with keeping him in my back pocket until I secured Karter, but since I basically did already, I didn't need him anymore.

Since that night we had sex, I saw Karter at least once a week. I know it wasn't a lot of time, but the fact that he made some time for me meant a lot to me. We weren't at the stage where he was cashing out on me yet, but I felt like we were getting there. My feelings for him were growing day by day and that was something I didn't really intend to happen. For example, when I found out that Lauriel would be meeting his family and going to his first game of the season, I was hurt and pissed.

Since it was an away game, I was hoping he'd ask me, but that was just wishful thinking. In my head, we would be in a different city, we could be out in public and no one would care. We couldn't do that here in New Orleans. When I questioned him about it, he said that his parents and siblings had been begging to meet his girlfriend and that was the perfect time to do so. I didn't care what his family wanted. I told him he needed to bring his real girlfriend and they didn't need to get too attached to her. He only promised to bring me to an away game this season.

This morning, I woke up knowing I would be watching my man on tv at home while his other bitch was in the stadium, screaming his name like she was the one that belonged there. I got pissed just thinking about it, which is why I made the fake page and created the post. It was petty. I knew it was petty, but I knew Lauriel. I knew she would see it and freak out on him. I was hoping she freaked out so much that she left his ass behind.

While I expected for a few blogs to pick it up, I didn't expect him to automatically expect that I did it. There were a ton of woman that would fantasize of being with Karter Montegue. Anyone could have done that. When Lauriel texted me, asking why I didn't check on her, I wanted to expose my own self. Instead of saying what I wanted to, I just decided to piss her off with my nonchalant attitude. She hated that shit and I knew she was mad because she didn't text back.

I wondered what she was saying to him right now. I

know he would never tell me, but I would know what happened by his willingness to see me. Or lack thereof. If he called me as soon as he got home, wanting some, she pissed him off. If I don't hear from him for a while, they're still hopelessly in imaginary love.

Knock, Knock

I got up to go answer the door. I wasn't expecting anyone because Noah had Nyjae were at Noah's parents house. When I opened the door, there was a piece of paper taped to the door.

I was shocked as hell when I opened it. "Eviction Notice??" Why the hell did we have an eviction notice? I know for a fact that Noah paid the rent faithfully. This had to have been some kind of mistake.

Picking up my cell phone, I dialed Noah's number.

"Hello?" He said in his deep voice.

"Why was there an eviction notice taped to the door?" There was no need to be pleasant. Me and this nigga didn't get along at all so it was no point faking it anymore.

"Yeah, and?" He said that shit so calmly. I pulled the phone away from my hear and looked at it like I dialed the wrong number.

"What do you mean, yeah and? Didn't you pay the rent?"

"I don't live there anymore. What reason am I paying the rent?" The audacity of this nigga.

"Motherfucker, me and your son live here. The least you could do is pay the bills. That's your responsibility." I couldn't believe Noah's punk ass. Since the night I didn't come home, he left the apartment and never came back. Shit, I didn't care not one bit because my man kept me satisfied. It was also a plus that he had Nyjae most of the time. I had so much time to myself. All I did was relax. I loved it.

"My responsibility? Nyjae is my responsibility. The day you decided you didn't have to bring your ass home like a woman with a man and a child at home was the day you were no longer my responsibility. Let's not forget you lied about your whereabouts."

"I didn't lie. I keep telling you, I was by Taniece's house."

"And I keep telling you that's bullshit and you know

it." We had had this conversation more times than I cared to admit and my answer never changed. He was adamant about me not being at Taniece's house, but he never told why. I didn't care because I was sticking to my story. Noah would find out about Karter one day, just not today.

"Look, bruh. That shit is neither here nor there. You need to pay the rent and you need to do it now." I didn't give a fuck about his attitude. I couldn't play my hand with Karter just yet because I didn't have the leverage to do so. I needed a little more time to get in good with him before I pulled a stunt like telling him I need a place to stay.

"The days of you telling me what I need to do are long gone. You are a grown ass woman. One that needs to get off her lazy ass and go find herself a job. I should have made you do that shit a long time ago, and I probably wouldn't have had to deal with the bullshit I dealt with."

"Get a job? Nigga, are you insane? I have a job. I'm a full-time mother." Can you believe this nigga started hilariously laughing on the phone like I told a Richard Pryor joke. I need to know what was so funny so I could laugh.

"What's so fucking funny?"

"You are. My nigga, you are fucking kicks. You really just said you're a full-time mother but barely have our son part time. Shit, you barely have him at all. Make that shit make sense." I rolled my eyes hard at what he said. Granted I knew I didn't have Nyjae a lot, but that was because he enjoyed being at his grandparent's house. Shit, I didn't mind. And now that his father was living there, he could stay there as long as she wanted.

"Look, Jream, I'm doing the back and forth with you. I'm going to pay the rent up for two more months. That'll give you some time to figure out your next move and getting on your feet."

"Yeah, whatever, Noah. Your no-good ass would only pay for two months." I was pissed. I didn't care if I didn't have Nyjae at all. I was the mother of his child. That nigga had full obligation to me.

"Bitch, I don't have to do nothing. You must have forgotten my name ain't on that fucking lease. I don't have to pay jack shit if I don't want to." When he said that, it made me calm down just a bit.

When we first moved into our apartment, Noah said he wanted me to feel secure. Like he wouldn't just put me out if his name was on the lease, so we only had the lease put in my name. Now that I think about it, that was the dumbest shit I could have ever did. Now I'm contractually obligated to pay this shit and he wasn't.

"Alright, Noah. Two months is fine." I hated I had to back down from this fight but I had to throw the white flag.

"Cool. Do you want me to drop Nyjae off later?" I really wasn't in the mood to run behind my son so I declined.

"No, he can stay with you and I'll pick him up from daycare tomorrow afternoon."

He laughed and said, "Yeah, right." Then he hung up dead in my face.

I was so sick of this nigga. I didn't know who this new Noah Baptiste was, but I needed him to get it together as soon as possible. I didn't care if we weren't together. I was used to him being at my beck and call. I expected it to stay that way. Until I had Karter exactly where I wanted him, Noah was still to do as I say.

He just didn't know it. Giving me that two-month time line lit a fire under my ass. I need shit to pick up and fast. So far, it felt like everything was working in my favor, but the results weren't happening fast enough. I needed a game changer and I needed it now. Something that would give me the control I needed to put me back in control of this situation.

Hopefully, I'd have my ace in the hole very soon.

*

It had been a few weeks since Karter's first game and shit was going well because they were undefeated. My baby was so pumped he had been seeing me at least twice a week now. I don't think he realized it, but he was getting really careless with his shit. He was coming to my apartment instead of us meeting somewhere. He would leave his phone just lying around. I don't think even he knows how many times I've cut it off when Lauriel was trying to reach him. I don't know what lies he told her, but she was believing them because they were still going strong. Much to my dismay, Karter kept telling me to be patient. How much more patient does a bitch have to be?

Shit, it seemed like he was feeding me the bullshit while giving her the happily ever after. But I couldn't believe that because he was straight up lying to her all the time to see me.

Right now, I couldn't even worry about those two. I was at the doctor for my annual checkup and I really wanted to get this shit over with. I may be a lot of things, but I make sure my kitty stayed intact. That was very import.

"Jream Daniels." Hearing the nurse call my name for me to make my way towards the back, I followed her through the doors.

"Good morning. Go ahead and step on the scale." I did as I was told.

"Ok, 135 pounds." After getting my weight, she went ahead and checked the rest of my vital signs.

As soon as she was finished with that, she handed me a small cup.

"Go right on in the bathroom and fill that up. When you're finish, put it in the window in the bathroom and go in room 5. You can get undressed from the waist down."

I went into the bathroom and filled the cup up. I used the sticker with my information on it and placed it on the cup. Then I washed my hands and went to the room that my appointment would take place in.

When I got in the room, I immediately got undressed and placed the paper cover over my lower body. While I waited for the doctor, I decided to text Karter.

Jream: Hey, baby. Am I going to see you tonight?

After only a few minutes passed, he finally texted back. I frowned at the response.

My Bae: No, not tonight. Spending time with L. ttyl.

The fuck did he need to spend time with her for. If he was breaking it off, he needed to spend less time with her and more with me. I was so fucking aggravated, I felt like I was about to lose my shit. Just as I was about to text back, the doctor walked in.

"Hi, Jream. How are you today?" She had such a perky demeanor and it was getting on my fucking nerves right now.

"I'm ok. How are you?" I wanted to keep it short and sweet so I could get out of here.

"Well, everything is good with me. But I am a little concerned about your blood pressure. It's a little on the high side and that's not good for the baby."

"Not good for the what?" I needed her to repeat herself.

"Oh, I thought the nurse had come in here and informed you that your pregnancy test was positive."

"No, she didn't. This is the first I'm hearing of it." I may have had a look of worry on my face, but I was smiling on the inside.

"Yes, Ma'am. Congratulations. You have a little bundle of joy in your belly."

"Can you tell me how far along I am?"

"Yes. I wanted to do that anyway because of your blood pressure. I figured I could do that and your pap smear all in one go. Give us a second to get the ultrasound machine." She walked out and left me alone with my thought.

I was pregnant. Man, I was so fucking excited. I had been wrecking my brain trying to figure out my ace in the hole and I finally had one. I knew how I got pregnant but because I didn't have any symptoms, I didn't think it was possibly working. See, Karter's biggest mistake was trusting my condoms. Every single time we had sex, I produced the condom. It was my act of showing him he could trust me. That shit was far from the truth.

"Alrighty, Ms. Jream. Let's take a look at the little bundle." Because we didn't know how far along I was, she did a vaginal ultrasound. As soon as she put that thing inside of me, she pressed a few buttons and we heard the heartbeat.

"Wow, our little one has a very strong heartbeat. Ok, from the measurements and the size of the baby, I can see that you're about eight weeks pregnant." I was doing jump and jacks in my head. Any fetus measured after eight-week gestation couldn't be terminated in the state of Louisiana.

"Thank you so much, doctor." She then did my pap smear and gave me a prescription for prenatal vitamins.

"The only thing I need you to do is stay stress free and check your pressure at least once a week until your next appointment. I'm going to schedule to see you four weeks from today. You have a great day."

After setting my appointment, I walked out of the

doctor's office with a huge smile on my face. I couldn't believe my plan worked. I was starting to give up on it, but that shit actually worked.

I knew I was in for some bullshit when I finally break the news to Karter, but I was ready for it. I was going to sit on this information for a few more weeks. I wanted to drop the bomb during the most necessary moment. I didn't know when that was yet, but I knew it would come to me.

Taniece

Since everything that happened between Noah and I, we had pretty much been avoiding each other like the plague. It happened months ago and neither one of us ever addressed it. I really did want to sit down with him and talk about it, but I didn't want to see disappointment on his face. Not disappointment in me, but in himself. I didn't want him to think he took advantage of me because that was farthest from the truth. He had actually made me feel more alive than I had felt in a while. Even though I hadn't had sex since then, my body was craving it. I wasn't craving it from just anybody. I wanted it from Noah. I knew there was going to come a time when we were going to need to talk about it, but now wasn't the time.

Today, I was meeting my sister and cousins for lunch. It had been on my heart to tell Lauriel for a while now, but I didn't know how to. She was one person, besides my mama, I didn't want to disappoint. Her opinion meant everything to me and it would remain that way. We had all decided to meet up at Houston's of New Orleans and I couldn't wait. We had been so busy with building Lauriel's brand and getting more business, we didn't have much time for socializing.

I guess I was the last one to show up because they were all seated when I got there.

"Hi, family," I greeted everyone.

"Hey, sister. What happened where you're just getting here? I thought you were done with your work."

"Yea, I was done with my morning work. I wanted to get a head start on the things I had waiting for me when I get back." My sister knew how I was. I was very organized. I didn't like procrastinating and I put myself on a schedule to get everything I needed to get done in a timely manner.

"Have y'all ordered yet?" I was starving and ready to eat now.

"No. We decided to wait on you," Keshyra said, looking down at her menu.

I noticed that my sister and Key were giving their full attention to their menu while Duchess was staring directly at me.

"What are you looking at?" I asked sternly. He knew I

didn't like that shit.

"I'm looking at you, hoe. There's something different about you. I can't quite put my finger on it." He was sitting his seat, tapping his perfectly manicured finger against his lips.

"Leave my damn sister alone. She don't have time to deal with your theatrics today, Darryl." I looked at Lauriel with wide eyes. She knew better than to do that shit. He couldn't stand his name. One, because he didn't think it fit him as a person, and two, because he was named after his dead-beat ass daddy. Long before he became Duchess, he hated to be called by his government.

"Oh, Bitch, you really trying it today. I wasn't even talking to you, mosquito bite chest having ass. I was talking to Taniece. Mind the business that pays you." Key and I both tried to stifle our laughs. I didn't want to laugh because my sister had just taken up for me, but he wasn't really lying. The big breast gene skipped right over Lauriel and came straight to me.

She stuck her middle finger up and rolled her eyes at him. Then she looked at me. "So, you laughing? I bet I never save your ass from him again."

I couldn't help it anymore. My laugh came flying out before I could stop it.

"I'm sorry, sis, but that shit was funny." Key and I were wiping tears out of our eyes.

"Un uh, Miss Thing. I'm not off your ass. What's up with you? I watch your ass when you walked in here. You got a new swing in your step." He looked at me through squinted eyes. "Let me find out you done finally gave somebody the kitty." Why did he have to say that when I was in the middle of drinking my water. I nearly spit it out all over the table.

"Nigga, stop playing with my sister. I'm tired of telling you, Duchess. Taniece hasn't given anybody anything," she said then looked at me.

"Well, let her tell me that. You ain't gave nobody nothing, T?" He could tell I was getting uncomfortable yet he didn't care. When his messy ass wanted the tea, he didn't let up.

"Duchess, leave her alone. This isn't something she wants to talk about in a room full of people," Key said. I could tell she was tired of her brother's antics. She adored her brother, she really did. She just hated how he acted sometimes. He just didn't know when to quit.

I was really thankful for Keshyra stepping in for me, but I knew if I wanted to tell them the truth, now was the only time I would have the nerve to.

"Not that it's any of your business, Duch, but yes, I've had sex." My sister jerked her head in my direction so hard, I thought it would have fallen off.

"You did what? With who?" They were firing off questions one by one.

"I knew it. I know my baby cousin. Her ass was walking like she had gotten some good dick."

"How did you know that? It happened months ago." This nigga had to be physic or something.

"Baby, it only needs to happen one time for your body to adjust to what it's not used to. That's what happened to this one over here," he said, pointing to Key. "The moment she lost her virginity, I knew."

"You didn't know shit. You were guessing and I told you. You so fucking dramatic."

"I'm just waiting on you to tell me who it was with. You didn't even tell me you were seeing somebody," my sister said while staring at me.

This was the part I didn't know if I wanted to share. I knew it would be hard for me to explain how it went down, but this was my sister. She would definitely tell me if I was wrong, but she was going to ride with me regardless.

I sighed heavily and said, "It was Noah."

"It was who?" She said angrily. I knew she wouldn't like it but damn, I didn't think she'd get mad at me.

"I said it was Noah." Duchess had a messy ass smirk on his face.

"Fine ass Noah?" He paused. "Lauriel's best friend's man, Noah?" He paused one more time for dramatic effect. "Jream's baby daddy Noah? Hot damn."

"Yes, that Noah." This dude was getting on my nerves.

"Taniece, what the fuck were you thinking? Why would you sleep with someone else's man, but worse, you gave him your virginity?" She said in a harsh whisper. She was trying to keep from yelling.

"Look, Lauriel. You have no clue what happened nor

how it happened. So, keep that judgmental shit to yourself." This is why I didn't want to go in deep detail. I wasn't about to sit here and she come down on me when I already did that to myself. Not because I gave him my virginity, but because I didn't wait until he was single.

"Are you the reason they broke up?"

"What do you mean they broke up?" Now that was news to me. I didn't know that nor had I asked my sister anything about Noah nor Jream. The most I had asked as it pertained to them was if she knew how my stanka man was doing.

"They broke up a couple months back. I don't know the details but sounds like it could have a lot to do with you." She sighed heavily. "How do you think that shit looks? My little sister sleeping with my best friend's man?" She was really starting to piss me off. I didn't give fuck how it looked because Jream wasn't my friend. I have never liked the bitch and I never faked like I did.

"This is some Kardashian, Blac Chyna type shit. Where the fuck is the popcorn when you need it?" Duchess wasn't making this shit no better.

"I'm about to call Teedy Vera to get your ass in check. It's your fault this shit even came up." While Key and Duch went back and forth, Lauriel just looked at me.

"What?"

"You're not ashamed of yourself?"

"Ashamed for what? It happened one fucking time. He and I haven't even talked about it since."

"Taniece, that's even worse. You let that nigga treat you like a slide." Now I was beyond pissed.

"Damn, Lauriel, that wasn't even called for."

"Nah, Key, don't tell her shit." I got up to start gathering my things. I wasn't staying here to take this shit from her.

"But let me enlighten you right quick. The night it happened, that shit was not intentional. Noah came to my house looking for your so-called best friend after she told him she was going to be at my house then block him from calling. I watched this man sit on my sofa feeling like he was the worst nigga alive because that bitch Jream made him feel like it. When he kissed me, he caught himself and tried to stop, but I kept going. I begged for it. I asked for it. I loved every minute of it and don't regret a damn thing. So, while you jeffing so hard for your best friend, ask that hoe where she was that night she supposed to be at my house while her man was fucking the shit out of me." I threw up the Deuces and got the fuck out of dodge.

Before I could make it too far from the table, I heard Duchess tell my sister, "You know you're wrong."

This time it wasn't in a messy tone. He was serious. I knew he was about to get her together, but I didn't want to hear shit when she finally reached out to me.

*

I was straightening up my apartment, waiting for my houseguest to arrive. The day I left after that terrible ass lunch with my family, Noah had reached out to me out of the blue. He apologized that he was just calling me; he had a lot going on. I understood and I didn't hold it against him. I was silently preparing myself for this conversation.

I decided that I would finally tell Noah how I felt about him. I was tired of carrying that burden on my shoulders and I needed to let it out. After all that had taken place, I would honestly be ok if he didn't reciprocate my feelings.

But I did feel like he needed to know my feelings.

Knock, Knock

Taking a deep breath, I went to answer my door. There he was. The handsome Noah Baptiste. He didn't look anything like he did when I last saw him. He looked stress free. He looked happy.

"Hey, girl. Long time no see." He reached in to hug me and I allowed it. He felt and smelled so damn good.

"Hey. How are you?"

"I'm actually good. The last few months has been exactly what I needed to get my shit together and to get some shit in motion." I smiled at him because he seemed like a better Noah. I liked that.

"Let's cut the small talk. I came over here because we need to have a long, overdue conversation."

He was looking at me like he was looking in my soul.

"I know. I was just waiting for when you were ready."

"I really appreciate that about you. You didn't hound me for answers that I didn't have. You weren't trying to make me say something that I didn't mean. That shit meant a lot to me."

"I knew that night was heavy on both of us. It was unexpected. Before you and I go any further, I want to apologize for not telling you that I was a virgin. I wasn't forthcoming with that information and that was fucked up. But Noah," I said and grabbed his hands. "I need you to know you didn't take advantage of me. Everything that happened that night, I wanted to happened."

In that moment, it felt like he let out a sigh of release.

"I'm so fucking glad you said that. A nigga was walking around feeling guilty as fuck thinking I stole your innocence from you." It was like he had a quick thought. "I have to ask, T, why me? Of all the niggas in the world that would love a woman like you, why me? Especially with all my baggage."

Now was the time for me to be honest about my feelings.

"Noah, I've been attracted to you since the night you met Jream." He looked at me with a shocked expression. "The night she approached you, I had just pointed you to them telling them how fine I thought you were. I had even said I was going to talk to you. She beat me to it. I was pissed."

"Are you serious?"

"Dead serious. I hated Jream after that night. Then when she would bring you around and I got to know your personality and watching the father you are to Nyjae, my attraction intensified."

"Why didn't you say anything? You could save me a lot of heartache and headaches?" He said with a laugh.

"How could I? I would never step on the toes of another woman no matter how much I disliked her. That's why it was so easy for me to give myself to you that night you came here looking for her. Noah, I see your heart. You're a damn good man. I just wish you had someone that could really appreciate you." I was tired of biting my tongue about Jream. I wouldn't go into full detail about the bitch, but I wouldn't hold back how I felt.

"You know what's crazy. She still maintains that lie that she was here. And every time she'd asked how I know, I wanted to say because I was there all night. I wanted to but I just wasn't ready to.

I put my head down and said, "Yeah, I understand."

Noah put the tip of his finger under my chin and said, "No, baby. Not because I was ashamed. I don't regret anything that happened that night. I only regret that I wasn't a single man when it did happen." He paused then said, "If we're laying everything out on the table, I had been attracted to you for a while. So much so, the only time I would last in the bedroom with Jream was if I was thinking of you. Shit, I didn't know what was going on with me but I do now."

"What's that?" I prayed his answer was something I wanted to hear.

"Taniece, Jream and I broke up the night we happened. Baby, I wasn't ready to come tell you how I felt, but I need you to know. I feel something for you. Something strong. I love how ambitious you are, how smart you are and the fact that you love my son. I don't know where this shit is going, but I'm ready to find out if you are."

My heart was beating outside of my chest. This was the shit I wanted to hear and had been waiting to hear. I just had one question.

"What about Jream?"

He looked at me like I was crazy. "What about her? I knew for a while that Jream wasn't the woman for me. She didn't love me for me, she loved what I could do for her. The fact that she didn't give a fuck about me doesn't change how I will treat you. If we get to that point, one day, I'll give you the world."

I was trying not to cry.

"I can't wait."

As soon as those words left my mouth, Noah kissed me hard like he missed everything within me. I know I missed him. I swear, I never thought this would happen, but I prayed the love God had for me was on its way. It may not be ideal but it was mines. And whatever bullshit was coming our way, I prayed we faced it together.

Karter

A nigga was exhausted. Between games, practices, endorsements and juggling two women, I was pass exhausted. At first, this shit was fun and games. I had successfully flipped the script on Jream. She no longer had blackmail on her mind; she had fallen in love with me. All she could talk about was when we would be together. I was tired of keeping up that lie.

I was feeding her bullshit to keep her in my back pocket, but after that stunt she pulled making that post, I knew it was time to let her ass loose. This shit wasn't any fun anymore and the guilt was too much for me. I knew I was doing suspicious shit that made Lauriel look at me funny, but she never questioned me. That let me know she was putting her all into trusting me. My bullshit was starting to catch up to me and I couldn't imagine losing my girl.

I had just pulled up to Jream's apartment to break the news to her. That's another thing. A nigga had started getting sloppy. Ain't no way I should be at this bitch apartment. I was slipping big time and I needed to get my shit together. Before I could fully knock on the door, she opened it with a big smile on her face.

"Hey, baby." She reached in to give me a kiss and I side stepped her. She looked at me strangely.

"Hey, wassup? Are you busy? Can we talk?" I looked around her apartment and I saw boxes everywhere.

"Uhh, yea, I'm just boxing up some of Noah's stuff. What's going on?"

I decided to just come out and say it. "Look, I know we been kicking it for a while now, but this shit got to end."

She looked like I knocked the wind out of her.

"It's got to end. The fuck?"

"Yeah, man, I can't do this shit anymore. I've been fucking over my woman with her best friend and that shit is eating me alive."

"Nah you're joking. You don't mean that, baby." She started walking towards me.

"No, I do mean it." I looked at her seriously. "I told you from jump that I loved Lauriel. I love her more than I need air to breathe. I honestly should have been done with you."

"What about you asking me to be patient? You said all I had to do was be patient," she was saying barely above a whisper.

"Look, Jream, I mean what I'm saying. This shit is over." I pulled out an envelope that contained fifty thousand dollars. I put it on her table.

"I know this probably doesn't make up for the hurt you feel, but it's something to say I'm sorry." I moved to make my way to the door.

"More like something for me to keep my mouth shut." I honestly wasn't going to say it but fuck it, she figured it out on her own.

"Well, yeah." Without waiting for a response, I made my way out of the door.

Fifty thousand dollars was a lot of money to just being giving somebody, but it was well worth it for her to shut the fuck up. I didn't give a fuck how much money I had to spend, I wasn't losing my baby for a fucking soul. Hopefully, Jream got the message loud and clear.

*

I was so happy we had a bye week this week because I had missed coming to Sunday dinners. My baby would always have a big ass plate waiting for me, but it was nothing like being in the presence of Ma Vera and Teeny Boo. Those two held a space in my heart forever and always. As soon as they found out I wasn't from here and had no family here, they treated me like I was a part of the family. Lauriel didn't even need to be around for me to be at either of their houses just shooting the shit. Even my mama loved them. She hadn't had the chance to meet them yet, but she was appreciative that someone was looking after her baby boy. Hopefully, I could make that meet up happen really soon.

We were all chilling in Ma Vera's living room watching the other games for the day. The food was ready. We were just waiting on Teeny Boo, Duchess and Keshyra to get here. My baby was sitting in my lap with a sad expression. She told me about the fight she had with Taniece and I told her she needed to squash that shit. She didn't need to be defending Jream for shit, but nobody could tell her nothing about that girl.

Now, I know what Lauriel had told T me did, but imagine my surprise when we got here and we saw Taniece sitting in Noah's lap talking to Ma Vera. Lauriel was pissed. She was about to say something, but her mother told her to mind her business. Ma Vera didn't play that shit. If she said something, you better listen. One time I cursed by accident and she slapped me with a ruler. I don't even know where the ruler came from.

"Hey now! Teeny Boo in the house!" This lady strutted in this house with her own personal style. I loved her because she was her true self and dared a motherfucker to question her. When my baby saw her, she put her head down and shook her head.

Teeny Boo was wearing a leopard print spaghetti strap cat suit with a black boa and some black flower flip flops. If they didn't share features, I wouldn't believe her and Ma Vera were sisters.

"Yasssss, Mama, you better work it, girl! Ya'll better not play with my mama." Duchess came in bucking his mama up. They were hilarious together.

"Would you two hush up? Damn, ya'll just got here

and you already starting. Where is my niece?" Ma Vera came out of the kitchen and asked.

"She had an assignment to finish, she's going to be here a little late."

"I swear, that's my sane baby. I don't know where I went wrong with you two." Duchess started laughing and walked over to Ma.

"Aww, Teedy, you know you loooooove me," his dramatic ass said. He looked in T's direction and I saw them messy ass wheels turning in his head.

"Well what do we have he-" Before he could finish, Teeny Boo popped him in the back of the head.

"Nah, nigga. I know you're going to leave my niece alone. Mind the business that pays you and carry your ass in the dining room." He looked like he was pissed he got popped, but he knew better than to say something. He ain't want Teeny Boo and Ma getting on his ass.

"Come, everybody, dinner is ready." I slightly pushed Lauriel off me because I was ready to eat. When we got to the dining room, I pulled out Lauriel's chair and then sat in mines.

"Lauriel, lead us in prayer," her mama said.

"Lord, we thank you for this food we're about to receive. We pray that it nourishes our bodies. Bless the hands that made this meal and continue to bless them as they make any other meal. Lord, we pray for everyone in this world, even those who don't believe. We pray no one goes untouched. We ask all of this in Jesus name, we pray. Amen."

"Amen," we all said in unison.

"That was beautiful, baby," Ma Vera said to Lauriel.

"It was just something that was on my heart." When she said that, I just looked at her in awe. I'm not gonna front, I had been screwing up a lot lately, taking this shit for granted when it was the greatest love I'd ever experience. Listening to my baby's prayer just further let me know I was making the perfect decision.

"Excuse me everyone." They all picked their heads up and looked at me.

"I know everyone's ready to eat, but I have to say something that's on my heart." I paused than took a deep breath. "When I got drafted to the Saints, I never expected that I would meet a beautiful woman and fall hopelessly in love with her. Much less, get accepted by the most loving family I ever met besides my own. I really just want to thank you guys for treating me so well and loving me so strongly."

Everybody started saying you're welcome.

Then I looked at Lauriel. "Baby, you came in my life so unexpectedly but you were exactly what I needed. You push me, you love me, shit, you make me want to be a better man. You have me thinking about the kind of legacy I want us to build for future. So, with that said." I stood up to pull the ring box out of my pocket and got down on one knee.

"Lauriel Mathers, would you do me the honor of being my wife?" I opened the box and it was a seventeen-carat, pear shaped, diamond ring. One day when were at the mall, I saw her eyeing something similar, I just bought a bigger version.

All the ladies had tears streaming down their faces. Even Taniece was crying. Even though she was upset with Lauriel, I knew she'd be happy for her sister.

"Damn, baby, you haven't said anything."

She started wiping her face then said, "Ye-" She was cut off by Jream.

"What the fuck is this shit?!" Jream screamed in the doorway of the dining room.

"What the fuck are you doing here?" Taniece asked, completely forgetting she was sitting in Noah's lap.

"Ms. Vera invited me when I saw her at the store." Taniece jerked her head in her mother's direction. "But the better question is, why are you sitting in my baby daddy's lap?"

"That's none of your business," Taniece said with the roll of her eyes.

Jream laughed and said, "For once, you're right." She looked towards me and Lauriel. "I'm more concerned with why my newest baby daddy is proposing to his old bitch." She shocked me with that shit.

"You're newest baby daddy? Karter, what the fuck is she talking about?" I couldn't even look Lauriel in the eye. My shit had finally caught up with me.

"Oh, he didn't tell you? Girl, your man been fucking

me for months now. I just hope he's ready to be a daddy," Jream said as she was looking at her nails.

"Bitch, shut up!" I had had enough of her fucking mouth. I looked toward Lauriel and said, "Baby, that bitch is lying."

Lauriel tried to jump up and go after Jream. I grabbed her to stop her. She smacked the shit out of me. "Don't fucking touch me!" She damn near screamed

"Jream, you need to go," Ma Vera said in a pissed of tone.

"Oh, I'll leave, but first I have one thing to say." She looked at Noah and said, "Baby daddy, you remember that night I told you I wasn't coming home because I was staying at Taniece's, I was with this nigga." She pointed at me. I looked at Lauriel and it was like the night I stayed out all night played back in her head. She just closed her eyes and shook her head.

Jream started laughing like this shit was a big fucking joke.

"You kept saying I wasn't there that night. Too bad you couldn't prove it," She said to Noah.

"Oh no, Bitch, he could prove you weren't there." Taniece looked at Noah and he nodded his head. "He came to my house looking for you, you dumb bitch. Instead of going out to actually find you, he used his time wisely and made love to me." Now Taniece had a smirk on her face.

Jream's eyes were bucking out of heard but no words came out of her mouth.

Needless to say, Sunday Dinner was a disaster.

To Be Continued...

About the Author

Brittany Nicole is a thirty-year-old young woman that has always had a passion for writing. She is from a small town of Louisiana called Reserve. She started writing poetry at thirteen and self-published her first novel when she was twenty-three years old. She is the mother of two handsome, little boys. Being a full-time mother and working woman derailed her dream for a little while, but now she's ready to make her dream come true full force. With grace and faith, she's determined to become your favorite author.

To submit a manuscript to be

considered, email us at

submissions@majorkeypublishing.com

Be sure to <u>LIKE</u> our Major Key
Publishing page on Facebook!